Stolen

Twin Moons of Andove
Book Two

Cassandra Logan

Stolen
Book Two in the Twin Moons of Andove Series
By Cassandra Logan
Copyright 2015
Cover created using Canva.com

Plot Synopsis

Sasha has just found out that she is not from Earth, that she can shift into a lioness, and, oh yeah, she's a princess. To say things are a bit complicated is an understatement, the last thing she needs is to find her mate.

Dax loves women and they love him. After watching his best friend Zeke go through a mating, Dax doesn't ever want to find himself chained to one woman. That all changes when his cat lets him know that Sasha is theirs.

Unable to resist their growing attraction they find themselves thrown into a political war that could end in death. Their deaths. Will they be able to survive? Or will Sasha's family kill them both?

Disclaimer- This story has several graphic sex scenes and some mild language

Prologue

Sasha was asleep in bed, sheets tangled around her feet where she'd kicked them. Arms thrown out taking up the entire queen size bed, as only a woman who had worked herself to exhaustion could. She was so deeply lost in sleep that when a man materialized in her bedroom, she didn't notice. She continued sleeping right up until the moment he reached out and touched her. Her eyes flew open and her fists shot out, but she was too late. He had already successfully ported her away from her bed and into a strange room.

Her eyes swept around the space, taking in the bare metal walls, the hard metal floor, and Anika, her best friend, pounding on the only exit. The noises coming from her were far from human and scared Sasha more than her new surroundings did. Earlier that night she'd found out that not only was her best friend an alien, but she could shift into a fairly large wolf. She hesitated before walking over, she'd never been afraid of Anika and deep down knew that Anika would never hurt her, but the noises she was making were terrifying. Sasha had never considered herself a coward, so shoulders back she marched over to where Anika was pounding on the door.

Her hand was barely on Anika's shoulder when her friends head whipped around. Her face was a mask of rage, but that wasn't what scared Sasha, it was the crystal clear blue eyes of Anika's wolf that were staring out at her. She snarled and Sasha could see the sharp canine teeth that filled her mouth. Slowly backing away, hands out, doing her best to remain calm, but barely containing her instinct to scream Sasha said, "Anika, honey, it's me, Sasha. You need to calm down, okay?"

She kept backing up and Anika stalked after her until she hit the far wall and could go no further. Anika walked right up to her, pressing her into the wall and then Sasha's eyes widened in terror when she felt the sharp bite of teeth against her throat. They didn't puncture her skin, but all it would take was the slightest bit of pressure.

She whimpered, she knew Anika wouldn't hurt her, but she wasn't sure about her wolf. Anika's growls stopped, and then she quickly backed away. Sasha's hands went to her throat, her eyes closed and a sigh of relief came rushing out. When she finally opened her eyes again, she saw Anika standing across from her. Eyes and teeth now fully human. Hand still at her throat she asked, "Are you ok?"

"I should be asking you that. I'm so sorry. You startled me and then when you backed away it was instinct the go after you." Her shoulders slumped and she refused to meet Sasha's eyes. "I'm sorry," she whispered.

Walking over Sasha pulled Anika into a tight hug. After a second Anika's arms went around her and squeezed back. "It's ok wolf girl. These things happen when you're an alien."

Anika gave her a skeptical look. Sasha just shrugged her shoulders, "I'm just guessing, but it seems like something that would be normal for you now. We'll have to ask the boys when we see them next."

Anika turned back to the door she'd been pounding on, "If we see them. That door is not budging and I'm not even sure we're still on Earth."

It was Sasha's turn to be skeptical, "If we aren't on Earth where are we? The moon? Mars? Did Martians kidnap us?"

Her eyes sparkled with mischief having too much fun thinking up possibilities. It helped keep her mind off the fact that she had been kidnapped from her bedroom and instantly transported to a small metal room.

"Worse. Ajax."

Anika stalked back over to the door, her fingers tracing the outline, trying to get a hand hold to try and pry it from its frame.

"Ajax? As in your uncle? Why would he kidnap us?"

Sasha was confused; Anika's Uncle Ajax was an odious little man that had raised Anika after her parent's death. While Sasha did agree that he was the scum of the earth, why would he kidnap them? Realization began to dawn on her. When Anika had clued her in about being an alien, she had also mentioned that her parents were killed in front of her. Anika hadn't remembered any of that, though, until Doctor Klews had removed the inhibitor chip from her brain.

A sinking sensation settled in the pit of Sasha's stomach. "Anika, why would your uncle kidnap us?"

Anika ignored the question and just grunted. She had moved from prying at the door to pushing. It wasn't moving, but she continued to try. Finally, she let out an inhuman howl and turned from the door. She began pacing in the small quarters. Growls coming from around her snarled lips and her teeth once again sharpening.

Sasha wished she could growl to express just how frustrated she felt. She knew, even without Anika telling her, that Anika had gone to confront Ajax and now they were both locked in a room with an unyielding door. She wondered why Ajax had kidnapped her until the pressure of a headache began bearing down on her. Her hands went up to her temples and she rubbed, trying to relieve the pressure building there. Out of habit, she began her yoga breathing exercises and that's when it came to her. She would need Klews to confirm, but she was positive she had the answer as to why Ajax had kidnapped her.

While Anika paced and Sasha came to a realization that left more questions unanswered than answered, a swirl of light appeared in front of the door and then a frightened young woman was standing there in her night clothes. The new woman's eyes went immediately to Anika and she moved away from her. Backing up until her body was wedged in the corner by the door. Her eyes nearly white in terror, she slid down the wall and curled up into a ball.

The surprise of someone else showing up in the room was enough to snap Anika and Sasha out of their own problems. Anika made a move to the new woman but when she let out a startled cry and began pressing herself even harder against the wall Anika stopped.

"Anika you're scaring her; why don't you move to the farthest corner? Try and give her some space."

Sasha knelt down in front of the woman, keeping some distance between them so she didn't crowd her. "Don't mind Anika, she's having some problems controlling her inner bitch."

Anika snorted at the comment

The woman was still terrified, but she no longer tried to melt into the wall. Her gaze darted between the two women. "Where am I? Please, I want to go home. Can you take me home?"

"I'm more interested in why we're here."

Sasha looked over her shoulder at Anika who just glared at her; she turned back to the scared woman. She moved to sit beside her, still trying not to avoid invading her personal space, but moving closer. "I promise wherever we are I will get you out of here and get you home."

The woman started to lose some of the terror from her eyes.

Then Anika decided to add to the conversation, "You can't promise that. Ajax is the one who kidnapped me originally. He's also the one who killed my parents, so there's no telling what he'll do." Her eyes took on the clear blue of her wolf and she looked at the woman cowering in the corner, "As soon as he comes back, though, I'm going to rip his throat out."

"Nice Anika. Really nice. Freak the poor thing out." Sasha glared at Anika as the woman began crying into her knees. Sasha moved over closer and pulled her into her arms. Hugging her; trying to soothe, but because of the growls that had started coming from Anika having very little success. She continued to hold the woman until her tears began to slow. "What's your name honey?"

"Kelly."

It was barely more than a whisper, but Sasha heard her. She pulled the two of them up so they were no longer sitting on the cold hard floor. She eyed the woman getting her first good look since she'd arrived.

She was small, barely 5'4", and curvy. Her eyes were almond shaped and a green almost hazel color, her hair was glossy black that hung nearly to her waist. She was wearing shorts and a t-shirt; her legs and arms were toned, she must spend her fair share of time in the gym. "Well Kelly, let's try and figure out what's going on. Can you tell me what happened before you showed up here? I was dead to the world in my bedroom until I felt a man slap something on my arm and then I was here. Is that what happened to you?"

Tears still trickling down Kelly's cheeks she nodded and sniffed. Her hands began trying to pull back hair that was falling in her eyes.

Sasha turned to Anika who had stopped pacing and was now standing in the far corner away from them. "What about you Anika? How did you end up here?"

Her voice, huskier than normal, she answered, "I went to confront Ajax, and kill him for what he did to my parents. When he answered the door, I attacked him. My wolf couldn't wait for his explanation." She growled, "He got away from me, he shot me with a tranquilizer gun and I woke up here."

She glanced at the other two women, Kelly was looking at her in shock and Sasha was deep in thought, she felt bad for getting them into this situation. Anika didn't know why Ajax kidnapped them, but she was sure he wouldn't have done so if she hadn't tried to kill him. Her arms wrapped around her body and she felt a deep sense of regret, her wolf only regretted not being able to kill him.

Sasha took a step toward Anika when the door opened and Ajax walked through. Anika made a rush for him, but he grabbed Kelly, wrapping one arm around her body and the other around her throat; he used her as a shield. Sasha pushed Anika back, "No! Anika stop, you'll hurt her."

Snarling behind Sasha, Anika kept back. Her eyes the cold blue of her wolf, she bared her teeth at him, peeling her lips back so he could see how sharp they were and imagine them ripping his flesh from his body. She growled, her voice low and gravely, "Why did you kidnap us?"

Ajax sneered at them from behind the frightened Kelly. "I didn't kidnap you. I took what was rightfully mine. I own each of you and I plan on finally getting a return on my investment. I knew the last time I spoke with you something had happened. It was just a matter of time before you fucked someone and then the profit from you would be halved. The people at auction want virgins, not used merchandise. Two out of three is better than nothing though." He leered at Sasha and pulled Kelly closer, squeezing his arm around her throat.

Sasha hated the fear she could see on Kelly's face as she clawed at the arm that was slowly cutting off her air. Sasha moved closer to him, hoping that she could figure out some way to get Kelly. Hands on her hips, she glared at Ajax, "If you think Anika is the only non-virgin here than you're in for a surprise. I haven't been a virgin since I was sixteen."

She wasn't prepared for the rage that colored his face and didn't see his fist until it was too late to duck. She fell back on the metal ground and her head landed hard on the floor, she saw black spots and then nothing as she slipped into unconsciousness.

Chapter One

Sasha walked through the lonely halls of the spaceship, following the scent she knew was unique to Anika. She needed someone to talk to, or at the very least something to do. She was going crazy just walking around this ship. How Zeke, Dax, and Klews survived all alone without killing each other escaped her. After the initial shock had worn off, and she'd begun to accept that she was an alien that could shapeshift into a lioness, the novelty of space flight, and even her situation, began to wear off. The fact that she also happened to be a princess was just something she tried to forget.

She was used to doing something, not just sitting around waiting, and that's all she'd been doing since she got on board. None of the knowledge she had transferred to her new world so she was just in the way and unable to help with anything. At least they were going after Ajax and Kelly.

It had taken some creative arguing on her part, but they were now on their way to a spaceport to begin the search. The men had wanted to take her immediately to Andove, their home planet, but she couldn't leave Kelly out there in the hands of Ajax. She had been sure Anika would be on her side, considering how much she wanted to kill Ajax, but something had changed between their rescue and when she saw Anika next. Three straight days of sex would dull anyone's quest for vengeance.

Sasha walked onto the observation deck; Anika was there with her easel set up and her paints out. She was painting space. What else would she be painting with that view? Stars streaked by just a blur of light as they flew. A deep, never ending darkness with stars sprinkled throughout. It sent a chill down Sasha's spine every time she saw it. Anika thought it was beautiful; Sasha thought it was disconcerting.

"I'm surprised to see you outside of Zeke's room, are you two sick of each other yet?"

Anika blushed, "No, the mating heat has cooled off some, though."

Zeke walked in just as she said those words and her blush deepened. He grinned as he walked over, "Tired of me already?"

Love and lust, in equal measures, filled her eyes when she looked up at him, they both forgot Sasha was there. Zeke's hand cupped her cheek, his thumb rubbing her lips. When his head dipped down to capture her mouth Sasha made her exit. She'd seen enough to know that this wasn't going to stop with just a kiss and watching her best friend have sex was the last thing she wanted to do.

Once again walking through the halls alone she tried to think of something that she could do, something to fill the time until they got to the space station. Nothing came to mind and as she started to prepare herself to spend the time alone in her room she spotted Dax. Rushing down the hall toward him, she grabbed his arm before he disappeared into his room.

"You have got to help me, Dax. I'm going insane. There is nothing to do on this ship! How have you not killed each other just to have something to do?"

Dax turned around and sighed, looking completely put upon. He leaned against the wall and stared down at her, "What am I supposed to do? I'm not shipboard entertainment. Didn't you bring anything with you?"

She clenched her teeth and tried to be nice, she didn't try very hard, though, there was just something about Dax that put her on edge. "No I didn't bring anything, I wasn't exactly given much time now was I?"

His smile just got cockier, it's like he knew he made her uncomfortable and he liked it. "You're the one that wanted to play hero and go after the damsel in distress Princess."

"Don't call me that!" Panicked by that one word her eyes were wild and she almost screamed at him. She had been raised in numerous foster homes and the news that she was royalty was impossible to accept. The idea of being a princess was too ludicrous to think of, she was rude, crude, and loud, on her best days. How could she possibly be a princess?

Dax saw her distress and he tried to think of something to say to make her feel better, but women and feelings were never his strong suit. He was more of the love 'em and leave 'em kind of guy. There was something about Sasha, though, she rubbed his cat the wrong way, and they both liked it. He cleared his throat and awkwardly patted her on the shoulder, "Um, it'll be ok. I'm sure your family will love you and if not you've always got Anika."

Eyes wide she tried to contain the horror she felt at that comment. She gave him a sick smile and croaked, "Thanks."

He could tell that he'd made things worse so he tried to back into his room and leave her in the hall, but her hand darted out to grab his sleeve.

"Don't go! I need something to do! Please, I'm desperate or I wouldn't be asking you for help."

Looking down into her pleading eyes Dax was once again caught by how striking she was. He'd seen more than his fair share of beautiful women, he couldn't help it if they flocked to him in droves. Sasha stood out among all of them; he couldn't quite put his finger on why though. She was tall and willowy, but her nose was too sharp and her eyes a little too big, all together it worked for him. He sighed and moved out of the doorway, "Follow me, I'll take you to the gym."

He turned and started walking down the hall, not waiting for her, just assuming she'd follow since she had nothing better to do she did. The smell of old sweat hit her nose when a door slid open to reveal a gym from the future. The equipment around the room was foreign and somehow familiar at the same time. He walked over to a panel on the wall and made some selections and music began pumping through the speakers. It took her a minute to recognize the lyrics but when she did she burst out laughing.

"You exercise to Psy? Really? A month on Earth and that's what you take away from it."

Grinning at her he changed the music and then walked over to a mat in the center of the room and began stretching. She went over to a machine that looked vaguely like a treadmill and began fiddling with buttons until she got it working. Once she had a steady pace she started to watch Dax. He had moved from stretching to doing some kind of martial arts. She studied his muscles, trying not to be obvious but having a hard time, as he flowed through the patterns. Being honest with herself she could admit that she was attracted to him. He was tall, muscular and had gorgeous eyes; the only problem was he knew it.

When she first met him she'd been struck by his looks, but after spending the afternoon with him, while Anika and Zeke had gotten to know each other, she'd had enough. He was gorgeous, but he was too cocky for his own good. She'd met his type before and while they were fun in college she was ready for a more serious relationship. Still, watching as he started doing vertical push-ups, the idea of a physical relationship didn't sound bad. In fact, it was starting to sound really good. Her inner lioness began to purr at the idea, in one hundred percent agreement.

Caught up in ogling Dax she missed her step and nearly fell off the treadmill. When she regained her balance the smirk on his face caused her to scowl. She increased the speed on her machine and blocked him out as she focused on her run. An hour later her legs were jelly as she stepped off the machine. Dax was still in the middle of his own exercise routine and to avoid getting caught ogling him again she made her way back to her room and took a quick shower in the bathing stall.

That had taken some getting use too. Evidently the people on Andove were very environmentally conscience, they also happened to have less water on their planet than Earth. So they didn't bathe with water they used some sound waves to clean themselves. It had been a strange experience to get used to but once she did she found it arousing. The invisible waves cascading down her felt like hands running over her body. Closing her eyes, she could almost see it in her mind. It was when she realized that those hands belonged to Dax that she knew she had a problem.

Stepping out of the shower she walked to the bed in the center of the room. Not bothering to put on clothes she fell back onto the cushy mattress. Staring up at the ceiling she tried to think of anything but Dax. With all that had happened to her it should have been easy to do, but her lioness wasn't helping matters. She wanted to find Dax and lick every inch of his body. As appealing as that sounded to Sasha, she knew that things would only end badly if she did. Past experience had taught her that if she slept with a man she had such strong feelings for she'd end up falling in love. She knew he was a heart breaker, the more she got to know him the more that knowledge was cemented in her mind, and she didn't have the time to deal with a broken heart, best to leave him alone.

Chapter Two

Dax watched as Sasha left the room and as soon as she was gone he collapsed. Gasping in air he groaned as his body refused to move. He'd already put in his standard four hours of exercise before Sasha had come to him asking for something to do. He never felt the need to try and impress a woman, but she was different. He couldn't figure out why but trying to impress her was leading him to stupid things. He'd provoked a fight with Zeke while on Earth and nearly had his head ripped off in the process, now he'd pushed his body harder than he should have. All to impress a woman.

He rolled over and slowly pushed himself up off the mat. Walking back to his room he passed Sasha's door and her scent drifted over him, painting an image of her in his mind. He fought down a moan and forced himself past her door and to his room. He glanced at the cleaning stall, wanting to wash the sweat from his body but not sure if he could take the feel of the sound waves right now. Losing control of yourself in a cleansing stall was something only adolescents did, but Sasha had him so on edge he was slowly losing control.

His panther wanted her and didn't understand Dax's hesitation in claiming her. That didn't help things in his opinion. His cat never paid attention to the many women he'd bedded. Having just watched Zeke's wolf drive him to the edge in pursuit of Anika the last thing Dax wanted to do was follow him down that same path. He wasn't ready to be pinned down by one woman, but his cat was telling him something else entirely. He growled and forced his panther down moving toward the cleaning stall, he was a grown man, a soldier, he wasn't going to let a woman cause him to lose control.

The next day his new resolve was already slipping. When he walked into the gym for his normal exercise Sasha was already there. She was running like she was being chased, watching her made his mouth water. Her smooth stride and the way her legs ate up the distance, he had to fight down a growl. He scowled and moved to the far side of the room where a punching bag was hanging. He spent the next hour trying to work out his sexual frustration. When he felt her leave he stopped his assault on the bag and leaned against the wall. He closed his eyes and inhaled her lingering scent. His panther purred and he groaned, he didn't need his life to be more complicated than it already was.

Moving back to the punching bag he'd only been working on it for a few minutes when Zeke's voice came over the intercom announcing their arrival at the space station. Dax jogged out of the room and to the flight deck where everyone was already waiting. Zeke was landing the ship while Sasha and Anika spoke quietly in the corner. Klews gave him a knowing look and he cursed the bear and his sensitive nose. Shooting him a glare he strode over to a console to check the security protocols he'd put in place. This station wasn't the seediest they'd been too, but it certainly wasn't the safest.

Once everything was in place and the docking clamps were secured he turned to the rest of the room. He and the other men had already discussed what was going to happen next, all they needed to do now was clue the women in on their plan. Something told him Sasha wasn't going to like it. He glanced over at her and she was doing her best not to look at him. The knowledge that she was having just as hard a time as he was fighting their growing attractive made him smile. When she caught that she glared at him which just made his smile grow, maybe he was thinking about this the wrong way. Maybe this could be fun. He certainly enjoyed seeing her pissed off.

Zeke cleared his throat and moved to stand by Anika taking her hand in his, he addressed both women, "Dax and I are going to go down to the station and meet up with a contact he has here. We need you two to stay here with Klews in case something happens. It's just going to be a quick trip to find out where Ajax has taken Kelly so we can get to her before she's auctioned off."

Watching Sasha as Zeke told them the plan, Dax could tell she wasn't happy, surprisingly she didn't resist, though. His estimation of her went up, he had been prepared to tie her down so she couldn't come with them. The two women would be easy pickings for the sort of aliens that frequented this station and the last thing they needed, while trying to get their information, was having to be on the lookout for kidnappers.

Once the plan was explained Dax and Zeke moved to the armory to suit up. Dax had knives and blasters hidden on every inch of his body and was just putting his tricked out helmet on when Sasha walked by them. Her scent surrounded him and was trapped in the helmet with him. He fought down a growl, he did not need her distracting him right now. He marched out of the room and fought his cats desire to search her out. The sooner they got the information they needed the sooner he could come back to the ship and start talking Sasha out of her clothes and into his bed.

The minute they stepped off the ship Dax knew that something was wrong. He scanned the crowd around him, assessing every threat and searching for the one he was missing. The station was not much more than a shanty town erected on a moon that had been classified devoid of anything of value. Those looking to survive under the radar had moved in and the place quickly became known as a collection of lawless aliens gathered from all across the galaxy. It was also one of the safer places to get information since people were constantly arriving and quickly leaving; news was always flowing. Dax had a contact from his days in the Andovian military and was hoping they could point him in the direction of the next slave auction.

Making their way through the crowds, they walked toward the edge of town and a small hole in the wall bar. Thankful for his helmet filtering out the stench of the dive, it took Dax's eyes a few seconds to adjust to the low light when they entered. He scanned the room taking in every heat signature that showed up on his helmets display.

Zeke walked up to the bar and was directed to a dark corner by the bartender. The alien in the corner had been trying to work his way up to being an information broker for years, with no luck. Dax had used him a few times for little bits of intel, but never anything on this scale. Sitting down across from him Dax noticed that time had not been treating him well. The aliens usual saggy dog face had even more wrinkles than the last time they'd met. His eyes were a bit too eager and Dax could tell he was even more desperate for the information broker title, hopefully, he hadn't done anything stupid.

The usual niceties had just gotten started when two women came crashing through the doorway, mercenaries hot on their heels. Ignoring the more than common occurrence, Dax was prepared to get down to business when he heard a small scream. Zeke was instantly on his feet charging to the aid of Sasha and Anika.

Normally Zeke wouldn't have had any problems handling a few mercenaries, but right behind them was back up. Zeke pulled the women behind him and growled at the men crowding in the door, he made sure to show his lengthening canines. Dax and his informant were still seated at a booth in the back on the bar. "Looks like your friend has his hands full." A raspy laugh followed those words; it was cut off when Dax pulled his gun out and aimed it at the informants head.

"I need an answer and I need it now. Do you know of any slave auctions coming up? Auctions were virgin Andovians are being sold?"

The man across from Dax licked his lips and his dark beady eyes studied the gun before moving back up to Dax's face, "There might be something. Information doesn't come cheap though. You know that."

Dax's finger began to tighten around the trigger and a squeak escaped from the now sweating alien. "You know I'm good for it, now as you can see I'm pressed for time and I need an answer now or I'll be forced to do something I really don't want to do. You wouldn't want that, would you?"

"No Dax, you know me. I can't let it get out that I give information out for free. I'm trying to build a reputation. I'll give it to you this time but don't go spreading it around. The only auction I've heard of is on an invitation only space station. It moves around, but last word was it was located near the Hunter's home world. I've got the frequency they use." He slowly reached down and with a few clicks the information began streaming across Dax's visor.

Standing up, Dax holstered his gun and with a few clicks of his own, funds were transferred into the informant's accounts. A sigh escaped the alien's mouth and he leaned back in the booth wiping the sweat from his brow. Dax was already moving and didn't notice his relief.

Zeke stood in between the women and the mercenaries, but they were creeping in on his territory and with his mate threatened he was starting to lose control of his wolf. The change was coming over him and a mist was beginning to rise. As soon as that happened he would be vulnerable to attack so Dax moved in beside him, putting himself in the way of any coming attack.

Just as the mist of change surrounded Zeke the men charged laser pistols drawn. Dax used his lengthening claws and swiped out at the closest mercenary, gouging deep scratches across his chest. Reaching for one of his guns Dax dodged a bolt and looked behind him to see how the women were doing. Sasha was standing guard over Anika as she completed her own change, Zeke's must have caused her to lose control.

His second of distraction almost caused him to take a laser bolt in the gut, but he quickly moved his focus back on the danger in front of them. Zeke was in wolf form cutting a path through their attackers, Anika close on his heels taking chunks out of anyone who tried to attack Zeke from behind. Dax moved back and grabbed Sasha throwing her over his shoulder and following them out of the bar and through the growing crowd of opportunists. Using his helmets communicator he updated Klews on their situation and told him to get the ship ready for take-off.

Once they were through the crowd Sasha started trying to wiggle off of his shoulder but he wrapped his arm around her legs and held her in place. He wasn't letting her go until they were safe on board ship and out of orbit. Then he was going to demand an explanation. His cat was anxious to make sure she hadn't been hurt and he was furious that she had disobeyed him. She could have been killed, or worse. Didn't she realize how dangerous space stations were? A little voice inside of his head told him she couldn't have known because no one had told her, but he ignored the voice, too angry to listen to reason.

Rushing up the rising gangplank Klews voice announced over the intercom that they were taking off but there were two ships already in pursuit. Dax noted Zeke and Anika still in wolf form as he charged past them with Sasha now screaming on his shoulder. On his way to the bridge, he dumped her in his bedroom and locked the door behind him. As he jogged away he could hear a soft thud as she pounded on his soundproofed door.

Ignoring Klews, he took his station behind the

weapons panel and focused on the two ships that were following them. As they left orbit one of the ships broke pursuit and headed away, jumping into hyperspace. One ship down, he locked on to the second waiting to see what would happen. He didn't have to wait long. Zeke was walking in zipping up his pants when they were fired upon. The ship shook with the force of the blow and Zeke called out that shield levels were down to 40 percent. Dax looked at the screen and then turned around to Zeke, "Drop the shields."

Zeke's stare was intense, but he reached for the control and did what Dax asked. Klews turned to both of them screaming, "Are you crazy?!"

Dax ignored him and waited. When the other ship saw their shields go down a hail came through. He opened the line but didn't respond. A booming voice came over the comms telling them to prepare to be boarded. With those words, Dax released one of the escape pods and the curses coming over the open comms followed by the ships instant pursuit meant that his plan had worked. Their attention on the escape pod Dax opened fire. The explosion of the enemy ship filled the screen and Zeke had them moving away and jumping into hyperspace before the blast impact reached them.

Clenching his fists, Dax fought down a growl when he turned to where Klews and Zeke were standing. He stalked toward Klews and grabbed him pulling him to his face, "Why the hell did you let Sasha and Anika out?" Zeke's growl joined his and Klews tried to pull himself out of Dax's grasp. Dax wouldn't let him move and shoved him against the wall, baring fang now.

Klews eyes began to turn red and his own chest began to rumble as a growl made its way out, "If you're implying that I'm stupid enough to let them off the ship then I resent that."

When Dax's grip loosened Klews pulled free and left the bridge, leaving Dax and Zeke both angry with no one to take it out on. Zeke took a deep breath and didn't even glance at Dax as he left the bridge to find Anika and make sure she was alright.

Chapter Three

Sasha paced inside Dax's room while her lioness paced inside her mind, both furious at being locked inside with no way to escape. It brought flashbacks to when Ajax had abducted her, the only thing that was keeping her calm was the fact that the rooms looked nothing alike. There was a large bed in the center of the room and she resisted the urge to tear apart the pillows that covered it. Dax also seemed to have an obsession with weapons. His walls were covered in them.

It was over an hour before Dax finally showed up but when he did she was ready for him. She stood to the side of the door and as he strode through she jumped on his back. She had briefly thought about using one of the weapons on the wall but decided that potentially blowing up the ship using something she didn't understand was not worth it.

Leaving the ship had been her idea, but as soon as Anika and she'd been spotted she knew they'd screwed up. Terrified of what would happen she had been desperate to get to Dax, she knew that if they could only catch up to him everything would be alright. The mercenaries just kept coming though, by the time they got the bar she had lost hope that they could be saved.

Watching as Dax had taken out the men and then when he grabbed her and raced back to the ship had been arousing, but when he'd just thrown her in his room and locked the door she'd become furious. Hearing over the intercom that they were about to be boarded had dampened down that fury but when nothing had happened and still he hadn't come back her lioness pride began to rear its head.

Now she was on his back biting and scratching, making him pay for abandoning her, leaving her without any explanation about what was going on. Before she could get a firm hold he flipped her over his shoulder and she landed on the bed hard, bouncing from the impact. Scrambling to get back up and attack him again she was too late and he straddled her, pinning her hands down to her side. She growled at him, her lioness starting to come out.

Eyes glowing Dax growled down at her, he lowered his head and sniffed her throat. She tensed underneath him until she felt him press light kisses along her jaw. He pulled his head back and looked down into her now glowing eyes. Her tongue darted out to wet her dry lips and his eyes watched the movement. Lowering his head, his lips hovering over hers, he waited just a second before pressing his lips to hers. She moaned and she parted giving him access to her mouth, his tongue invaded her, tasting her. Their scents combined with their growing passion. He moved her hands above her head so that he could hold them down with just one of his own, and used his free hand to start roaming across her soft body. He pushed her shirt up and his hand found her breast, cupping it, his thumb rubbed her hardening nipple through her bra.

A moan escaped Sasha's lips and she bucked

under his weight fighting to free her hands so she could move them across his body, across the muscles she'd been lusting after since she'd met him. No matter how hard she pulled he wouldn't release her hands and her resisting just made them both that much hotter. A growl escaped Dax's lips and a ripping sound filled the air as he tore her shirt and bra from her body. His mouth lowered and he gently nipped at her hardened nipple. Gasping she arched into his mouth as he began slowly swirling his tongue around her before nipping with his sharp teeth. While his mouth was occupied his free hand began working its way down her bare torso and to the top of her pants. His fingers made quick work of the button and zipper and within seconds her pants were slipped down around her knees. He tore her underwear off and then his hand paused before unhurriedly making its way up and past her small thatch of dark curls.

Now panting Sasha froze, waiting for what he would do next. Pulling back from her breast he stared intensely down at her. Trapped beneath him, he moved his hand slowly. Her head fell back on the bed and she moaned, desperate for him to move faster.

He started to chuckle at her impatience but his chuckle died in his throat when she lifted her head up and began nibbling on his ear, working her way slowly down his neck before she bit his collar bone. Making a moan of his own escape his lips. He used his fingers to part her intimate lips and he started easing one digit slowly inside of her using his thumb to draw circles across her clit. She bucked into his hand and she bit down harder on his collar bone. His grip loosened on her captive hands and she was able to pull them from his grasp. Hands-free she attacked his body, ripping his shirt off and baring his chest.

Growling at the loss of his hold on her hands, he removed his finger from her and started moving down her body until his mouth was over her pussy and her hands buried in his hair. He used his fingers to part her wet lips and then his tongue was on her, licking and sucking her clit while he began working his finger in and out of her slick channel. It had been so long since Sasha had let herself have any kind of sexual release and she'd been lusting after Dax for days now, she could feel an intense release building inside of her. She was just on the edge of her first orgasm in three months when he stopped. She fought down a scream of frustration.

Moving off of her Dax stood up beside the bed and leaned over to pull her jeans the rest of the way off and then he started stripping out of his own clothes. Standing in front of her, completely naked, cock thick and jutting out he looked down at Sasha, lying there, naked in his bed. He could feel his cat purring, telling him that this was meant to be, that she was his true mate. He was floored by the realization. They hadn't even dream walked, but there was no denying the conviction his panther was sending to him. He pushed the thoughts from his mind, focusing on the moment. On the pleasure he intended on giving and receiving from her.

Grabbing her legs he pulled her to the edge of the bed. He could tell that she was still close to orgasm she just needed one more push to come crashing over the edge. He leaned over her, he saw the anticipation shining in her eyes and when her tongue darted out to lick her lips his gaze dropped. Her lips were so plump and inviting. He could think of several things he'd love to have those luscious lips doing to him.

Impatient, Sasha grabbed his head and pulled him down, giving him a searing kiss that told him just how desperate she was to feel him inside of her. Tearing her lips away from his she growled, "Fuck me now fly boy or I'll go see what Klews is up to."

He could feel his eyes changing at her taunt and he moved back so she couldn't see. His panther was ready to run down the corridor to the medical bay and tear Klews apart at the very idea. Before she could notice the change and get scared Dax flipped her over onto her stomach and lifted her up so that she was resting on her knees ass in the air. He moved his hand to position his cock at her still slick opening and when she looked over her shoulder at him he drove inside of her, hard and fast, causing a scream of pleasure to tear itself from her lips. He pounded into her, the sound of their flesh smacking filling the room. When he reached down and began rubbing her clit the cry that came from her lips filled him with pleasure. Her walls began clenching around him and he fought to maintain control, wanting to make her orgasm last as long as possible before he came inside of her.

His panther so close to the surface because of her comment wanted to mate with her then and there. He eyed her shoulder as she started to come down from her orgasm and he knew all he would have to do is bite and it would start the mating bond. For a split second his panther and human sides were in agreement and that's all the time the panther needed to take control and lean down and make his mark. The taste of her blood and the beginning of the mating bond pushed him over the edge. He pounded into her as her screams of ecstasy filled the room and he let out a roar declaring that she was his forever.

Lying in Dax's bed Sasha couldn't believe how amazing that had been. For some reason the lioness inside of her, that she still had not yet had the courage to give control to, wanted to bite Dax. It wanted to bite him bad. She was still too fuzzy to think clearly and just pushed the strange thoughts away. Preferring to focus on what had just happened. She had been coming down from a very satisfying orgasm, her first in way too long, when she'd felt pain in her shoulder and then it was like a wild fire had coursed through her veins causing her to start climaxing all over again. Only this time it was like nothing she had ever experienced before. At one point, she had been certain she was going to die from the pleasure filling every pore of her body.

Busy focused on what she was feeling it took her a minute to realize that Dax wasn't in bed anymore. When she rolled over and looked around the room she discovered he wasn't even in the room. Momentarily shocked that he would just leave her alone in bed after giving her mind blowing sex she fell back and stared at the ceiling. She pressed the palms of her hands to her eyes and groaned. She knew it would be a mistake to sleep with Dax. She had been weak and now he'd gotten what he wanted and left.

Fighting back tears she rolled off of the bed and began pulling her tattered clothes on. She didn't plan on being there when he got back. She didn't want him to think that the sex had meant more to her than it had obviously meant to him. Thankfully his door wasn't locked this time and she peered around the door frame and looked down the hall to make sure no one was there, in her current state of undress the last thing she wanted was to run into someone and have to explain what had happened. She hurried through the passageways and quickly slipped into her room successfully avoiding contact with anyone.

Alone she dropped her tattered clothes in a pile and went to the shower stall. Too tired to worry about the effect the sonic waves had on her body she just wanted to be clean, and get be rid of Dax's scent.

Chapter Four

As soon as he realized what he'd done Dax eased out of Sasha's still quivering body and barely remembered to grab pants in his haste to get away as fast as possible. He could already feel their incomplete mating bond pulling at him, making his cock hard despite the fact that he'd just had the most powerful orgasm of his entire life. His panther wanted to go back and complete their bond; it knew that Sasha's lioness wanted them. The only problem was did Sasha herself want them?

He groaned and continued through the ship trying to get as far away from his room and Sasha as possible. He made his way into one of their empty cargo bays and began pacing, working to calm his body down so that he could think clearly. If she'd only been raised on their planet she would know what his bite meant and what her cat was more than likely telling her. They were meant to be, they were true mates. The fact that Anika and Zeke were both true mates as well wouldn't help him convey just how rare such a thing was but maybe seeing them and how much they obviously loved each other would help his cause. He hoped.

Growling he raked his fingers through his hair and tried to figure out what to do. If it was just their incomplete mating bond it would be one thing but, unfortunately, that was just the tip of the iceberg. Not only were they in the middle of a mission to find the kidnapped Kelly but there was also the fact that they needed to get Sasha back to their home planet to be reunited with her family, her Royal family. The same family that controlled the military that dishonorably discharged him for something he hadn't done. To say that things were complicated was an understatement.

His pacing became more frantic and instead of calming down, his panther was gaining control. Considering its main desire was to take Sasha and run, he needed to avoid that happening. Pausing in the middle of the cargo bay he unknowingly began emulating the same breathing techniques that he'd noticed Sasha using when she became upset. Minutes passed and finally he had a tentative grasp on his control. The first thing he decided to do was visit Klews and see if he had anything that would stop their mating bond, or at the very least dull the ache he felt growing.

Making his way through the ship he passed Sasha's room and judging by the strength of her scent he knew she was inside. He slowed as he passed and took a deep breath, filling himself with her unique aroma, torturing himself. He was just about to force himself past and to the medical bay when he realized her scent was filled with pain. He growled and strode back to her door. Not even pausing to knock he barged in just as she was stepping out of the cleaning stall.

"What the hell are you doing here?" She glared at him as she quickly pulled on clothes trying to cover her body from his sight. He frowned confused at her reaction, his eyes searched hers to see if she had any wounds that would be causing the pain that was coming off of her. His eyes quickly found the bite mark he'd left on her shoulder, it would leave a scar for all to see so they would know she was claimed, but it was already beginning to heal and shouldn't be causing the pain he could see on her face.

"Are you hurt? Why are you in pain?" He made his way to her so he could do a physical examination, but she moved around the room to get away from him. Had he hurt her while they'd had sex? He'd never caused a woman pain before while making love and the idea of the first being Sasha was almost too much for what little control he'd recovered from his cat. He paused and began slowly breathing trying to calm down so he could figure out what the problem was.

"I'm not in pain, I don't know what you're talking about. What I do know is I want you out of my room. You can't just come barging in whenever you please. Yes, we had sex, big deal. That doesn't give you the right to invade my privacy. I want you to leave right now." Her last words were said in a yell and her hands were on her hips as she glared daggers at him.

Completely confused Dax just stared at her. Didn't she feel the pull? The desire? He was having an almost impossible time not ripping off her clothes and continuing their mating right then and there, yet other than being obviously pissed off she was showing no signs of the same desire. Was it possible the mating was only going one way?

Horror at that thought filled him, he'd never heard of the possibility, but that didn't mean it couldn't happen. What if he was alone in this mating? He groaned and would have started pacing again, but Sasha had enough and was starting to physically push him from the room. As soon as her hands had touched his skin an intense fire of lust had coursed through his body and his cock grew hard. Starting to reach for her she gave one final shove and he was out in the corridor as her door slid closed.

Fists clenching at his side he fought down his desire to override her door locks and take her then and there, turning he made his way to his original destination. The medical bay. If anyone would know what was going on Klews would be the man. There was also the hope that he would have something that could help dampen down his craving for a particular lioness.

Minutes later Klews response to his request had him grinding his teeth and crossing his arms in a desperate attempt not to throttle the laughing bear. Wiping tears from his eyes Klews was starting to bring himself back under control but he lost it again when he looked at Dax. Another five minutes later and Klews was finally able to answer Dax's questions.

"First off I just have to say, it serves you right. With the amount of tail you've chased and the shit you gave Zeke about Anika, it was karma. Second, I've never heard of a mating bond only going one way. That's not to say that it can't happen, just that I've never read anything about it. I'll do some research and get back to you. Seriously though you have to tell her what you're going through. She wasn't raised on our planet so she isn't going to understand what's going on and the last thing you, of all people, need to do is piss off someone in the Feline Royal Family."

Dax turned away from him and began pacing in the small confines of the medical bay while Klews watched him. Dax knew what he had to do but telling a woman you were just getting to know that you were destined soul mates was kind of tricky. Growling he turned and left, he headed for the gym to try and work out his problems.

Hours later, exhausted and sweaty he was no closer to an answer. Zeke's voice came over the intercom calling him to the bridge just as he was getting out of the cleaning stall. Pulling on clothes he made his way to the bridge and entered just behind Sasha. He reached for her, but she was too fast. She moved to the other side of the room and stood as close as possible to Anika. She glared at him and then proceeded to give all her attention to Zeke, ignoring him. Dax ground his teeth and fought the desire to smash his best friends face in.

Standing in the middle of the bridge Zeke pretended not to notice Sasha's reaction to Dax, but his quick glance to Klews told Dax that he knew what was going on. It was impossible to keep any kind of secret on this ship. He crossed his arms and glared at his friends.

Zeke pulled up the information the broker had given Dax before they'd been forced to leave. It was just a frequency that the auction house was using but once Zeke plugged it into the ships navigation it showed the auction houses coordinates which turned out to be just a short jump away from the Hunter's home world.

Glancing at the other two men Zeke said, "This is going to be a problem."

The Hunters, or Zellims since their planet was called Zellim, were in a constant state of war. They loved the kill and the only way their government had found to control them was maintaining at least three active conflicts. Since the Hunters had discovered space flight they had been at war with the Andovians. The fact that they shifted into animals appealed to the Hunters, they saw an Andovian pelt as the ultimate trophy. It certainly explained why Ajax had kidnaped the three women, Andovian females were in high demand because the Hunters enjoyed raping them and then hunting them in their animal form.

Zeke continued, "The auction is going to take place in three days. Our best chance of saving Kelly is before she's sold. If a Hunter wins her our ability to rescue her afterward will be slim to none."

"Then what's the problem? Let's go save her." Sasha looked around at the men then at Anika who just shrugged her shoulders as confused as Sasha about what the problem was. "Am I missing something?"

Gritting his teeth Dax fought down the mating urge, burying his cat he growled at her, "We can't just go guns blazing and snatch her up. Not only will we have to bypass the auction house security, but we'll have to make it through all the customers there planning on bidding. There's also the fact that you happen to be the long lost Feline princess and if we take you anywhere near that auction we'll all be executed by your family. Do you get why we're not just running in now?"

She glared at him and he could tell that she was close to losing her temper, for some reason it flipped a switch inside of him and he began to calm down. This was his mate, he knew she was his, and he couldn't wait to convince her of the fact. He was actually starting to look forward to the process as he watched her anger grow. He shot her a cocky smile and that was all it took to send her over the edge and start screaming at him. Her anger proved that he affected her the same way she affected him.

"So because I'm some stupid princess we're going to leave this poor defenseless girl to fend for herself? Is that it? You're going to abandon her because you're afraid?" She snarled at Dax, ignoring the others on the bridge focusing all her anger on him. She stalked forward with each word until she was standing right in front of him her finger out poking him in the chest. She looked up at him and said, "I thought you were better than that Dax, but I guess I overestimated you yet again."

Her last statement pissed him off to no end and he opened his mouth to start his own loud argument, but Zeke stepped in before he had a chance.

"Enough. Sasha we don't plan on abandoning Kelly, we're going to do everything we can to save her. First, though, we have to make sure you're safe. If you're captured again it will cause a whole new set of problems that we really don't want to deal with. Since the auction is so soon there isn't enough time to take you to Andove and execute a rescue attempt at the auction house. The only option we have is to split up. We have a small ship that can take two of us to Andove and the rest will head up the rescue. There's also the added bonus that if something happens to the rescue party the two that went to Andove can act as backup. It will take about three days for each group to get to their destination. Once the mission is completed we'll contact you on Andove."

Sasha crossed her arms and frowned at Zeke. Dax could tell she didn't like the plan, but he wondered if she would realize that it really was the only way. Finally, she nodded her head in agreement. Suspicious he said, "Is that a yes you agree to Zeke's plan or are you planning something stupid like last time? Remember you didn't just put yourself in danger you nearly got all of us killed."

She glared at him, "If I had known how dangerous it was I wouldn't have snuck out. This time things have actually been explained to me."

Crossing his arms, he studied her and hoped that what she said was true, the last thing they needed was her trying to play the hero. If anything happened to her before they got to Andove then they were all dead. Of course he didn't plan on letting anything happen to his mate, still she had proven to be very strong willed and he doubted if he could stop her if she really set her mind to doing something. He decided not to let her know that though.

Chapter Five

Knowing that a plan was good didn't mean she had to like it, and Dax acting like she was going to do something stupid didn't make her any happier. Of course everything, Dax did pissed her off right now. Well maybe pissed her off wasn't exactly right. Everything he did seemed to be arousing her, and that pissed her off. She wanted to be angry at him, even hate him. He'd used her and then just left. The fact that he'd come to her room later asking if she was okay didn't make things better, it just confused her.

Now instead of being angry all she could think about was running her hands all over his naked, hot body. With just that thought her mind began to wander and everything she wanted to do to him began floating through her mind.

Quickly tamping down on her thoughts, she didn't want to let everyone else on the bridge know what she was thinking, and in a room full of shapeshifters that was easier said than done since they could smell the slightest hint of arousal. Gritting her teeth she brought her focus back to Zeke in time to hear him say that Dax would be the one accompanying her to Andove.

"What? Are you serious? I'm not going

anywhere alone with him." Desperate she looked to Anika to back her up, but the smile on Anika's face let her know she was on her own. "This is ridiculous! I'd rather go on my own than with him."

"No such luck princess. I didn't exactly leave Andove in the best of circumstances and the Feline Military have lots of reasons to not want me back. Still it would be better than a wolf or a bear bringing you back, and they'll need Zeke's tech skills and Klews medical knowledge to save Kelly. It sucks, but I'm the obvious choice to escort you."

Eyes wide at the prospect of spending any length of time alone with Dax she had to fight down the urge to scream. She could feel her lioness beginning to rise up inside of her, fighting to take over, she closed her eyes and began her breathing exercises still not ready to relinquish control to her animal side. She could feel the tension in the room as she fought for control and finally won. Hanging on to that control by a thread she growled at Dax.

"Let's get this over with. The sooner we leave, the sooner they can reach Kelly and save her."

Turning on her heel she left the bridge. In her room, she began throwing the few things she'd brought with her in a suitcase and muttered to herself.

"I can't believe this, stuck on a small ship with him for days. This is just my luck, but I will not sleep with him. Fool me once shame on me, I'm not going to give him the opportunity to fool me again."

Pausing in front of a small mirror in the room she stared at her reflection. She could see the almost rabid desperation in her eyes. She wanted Dax more than she'd ever wanted a man, it was actually causing sweat to drip down her back. She knew she was going to sleep with him, she didn't have the strength to resist this pull. Next time, though, she was going to remain in control. She would be the one leaving him alone, she wasn't going to give him a second chance to hurt her.

Bags packed she was ready to leave her room when Anika walked in. She hated goodbyes and with all the changes her arrival at Andove was bound to bring she didn't know the next time she'd see Anika.

"I know you. If I let you, you would have gone straight to the ship and just left without saying anything. But I'm not going to let you."

Stepping forward Anika pulled Sasha into a tight hold. They had been friends since grade school and so much had changed in such a short time, but now they weren't going to have each other to lean on. She put her arms around Anika and hugged her tight, fighting the tears. After a few minutes, Anika pulled back, wiping at her tear stained face she sniffed then frowned.

"Are you bleeding?"

Momentarily put off by the random question it took Sasha a minute to realize her bite wound must have reopened. She pulled her shirt down to inspect it.

"Shit. I thought it was healed, I must have broken a scab or something. I'll have Klews look at it before I leave."

Frowning at her Anika asked, "Is that a bite mark?"

Blushing she answered, "Yeah, I kind of had sex with Dax and he must have bitten me. Honestly, I didn't feel it at the time but it's pretty deep."

"Dax bit you? Oh my god. Did you bite him back?"

Anika looked concerned as she waited for Sasha

to reply.

"No, I'm not really into biting. Though my lioness kept trying to get me to. Why? It's no big deal."

"Yeah, it is Sasha. Biting is part of the mating ritual, it begins the bonding process and once you're mated you're mated for life. If Dax bit you it must mean that he really loves you because that's the only reason any of the guys would do it."

Shocked she backed away from Anika and said, "That can't be true. I mean after we had sex he just left me there. Mind blowing orgasm like I've never had and then he just leaves and doesn't say anything. I'm pretty sure love is not what he was feeling."

Anika looked unsure, she was still new to everything so it was possible she was wrong. Sasha shook her head and continued, "Maybe it's only a wolf thing. We're both cats it probably doesn't work the same way."

"I don't know. It's possible, but I don't think so. You should definitely talk to Klews about it, he would know, plus he can look at the bite mark and maybe give you something for it."

"I'm sure I'm right. There's no way Dax would bind himself to me, any woman for that matter. I know his type Anika, he loves to have sex with a woman, but he's not going to tie himself down to one."

"Still I think it might be a good idea to talk to Klews about it. He can give you a definite answer."

Grabbing her bag Sasha walked to the door and said, "I'll stop by the medical bay before I leave. I promise."

Smiling at Anika she quickly left before she got too emotional. It was better to focus on her future than to think about when she would see her best friend again.

Walking down the corridors she thought about what Anika had said, she was sure she was wrong. There was no way Dax had any kind of strong feeling for her. He just wanted sex that was all. But if it was true did she even want to be bonded to him? For life. Earlier she had thought she might be falling in love with him, especially after that amazing orgasm, but it was too soon for that. She was not the type of person to fall in love quickly. That was Anika, the artist. She was a lawyer, she was analytical and she didn't rush into things. Well, not important things.

Walking into the medical bay she had convinced herself that Anika was wrong and that things had to be different for cats. She was about to turn around and head over to the ships bay to board and wait for Dax when Klews glanced up from his desk.

Surprised he said, "Sasha, I thought you'd be getting ready to leave. Was there something you needed help with?"

Shifting between her feet, unsure if she wanted to ask a question she was pretty sure she knew the answer to, she decided she might as well go ahead since he was there.

"Actually yes, I was wondering if you could look at this bite mark I have."

Clearing her throat and working on not blushing she continued, "Dax and I sort of slept together and in the heat of the moment he bit me. It doesn't really hurt, but I thought it might be best to have you look at it."

Eyes wide Klews just stared at her.

"He bit you? I mean while you were having sex he actually bit you, broke the skin and everything?"

"Yeah. It's no big deal, it just happened. Like I said it doesn't hurt or anything I just thought it might be good to have it checked out before I leave."

Klews grin was filled with knowing and she blushed under his gaze as he pulled out a medical scan.

"I'm sure it didn't hurt. From what I've heard it probably felt amazing. Did Dax talk to you afterward? Tell you anything?"

He began running the scan as he waited for her response. She knew, even though he hadn't said anything, she knew that what Anika had said was true and she started to become frantic and lose control.

"Oh my god Anika was right. He's mated himself to me! How the hell can someone do that to a person? Do I even get a choice in the matter? What am I going to do? I can't stay with him. He's a player, he'll just cheat on me once he gets tired of me. This is horrible."

Her eyes were wide and she was working herself up to tears, her lioness was rising up trying to take over. She didn't realize it, but her eyes began to change color, when the mist of change began to swirl around her she fought for control and won. She could tell that her lioness was angry at being denied, though.

Klews had watched helplessly until she'd gained control.

"You'll have to let her out sooner or later, she's not going to take being kept inside much longer. The longer you put it off the longer she'll maintain control when you finally do let her out."

Wiping her eyes she said, "I'll deal with that when it happens."

Taking a deep breath she composed herself and asked, "What does this bite mean, exactly?"

He hesitated and her eyes narrowed. She put her hands on her hips and continued, "I need to know now Klews. From someone that isn't Dax, before I spend the next few days on a ship alone with him."

Putting the medical scanner away, Klews stalled for time while he tried to come up with a legitimate reason for Dax to explain what he'd put into motion. Unfortunately none came to mind and he was forced to do something that his friend should have done in the beginning.

"By biting you Dax marked you as his mate and started the bonding process. If you bit him it would have been completed."

She shook her head at his unasked question, now happy that she'd resisted the urge when they'd had sex.

He went on, "Since you didn't bite him, I'm not entirely sure what you'll experience. Normally when a mating starts the couple will spend days locked up together consummating their bond as often as possible. The urge to mate becomes all-consuming and that's all they can think about. That's what Anika and Zeke are just coming out of. Since you didn't bite him you're both probably experiencing an intense sexual draw and your lioness will want to bite him anytime you have sex."

He shrugged his shoulders and held his hands out in a helpless gesture, "Honestly that's all I know. When you get back to Andove the doctor's there will know more."

Eyes wide she tried to process what he was telling her but everything was still so new, she asked, "Is this permanent? Will it go away?"

He gave her a sad smile, "For you? I don't

know, possibly. For Dax, no. As soon as he bit you he sealed his fate."

Concerned she asked, "What will happen to him?"

"Don't think about it."

Eyes narrowing she glared at him, "Klews, answer me. If -- when we don't mate what will happen to him?"

Sighing Klews moved across the room straightening an area that didn't need it. "If an Andovian finds their true mate, which is incredibly rare and only happens when the animal side of us chooses a mate, but if they do and they begin the bonding process and then aren't able to complete it they die. Since you didn't bite Dax the process might not have started for you."

Skeptical she said, "So basically you're saying if he doesn't have a lot of sex, with me, that he'll die. Yeah, I'm sure. That sounds like a great big conspiracy that a group of men came up with." She crossed her arms and rolled her eyes at him.

He chuckled and shook his head, "No it's not a conspiracy, it's something that's been hardwired into us. It's not so much the sex as the closeness. We have to be with our mate during this time, it's a scent thing I believe. But then again this isn't my expertise."

"So he has to be near me or he'll die? How long? Days?"

"Until the mating is complete and the heat has worn off he needs to be near you. If you never complete the mating then he'll need to be near you forever, theoretically. It might not work, there might be more to it, but I just don't know."

Pacing around the room Sasha tried to wrap her

head around what Klews was saying. How could this be possible? Why would Dax do something like this if it could lead to his death?

"Wait you said that if it's a true mating, what is that exactly? Maybe it isn't, maybe it's just something he does during sex. Do you seriously see Dax doing something that would tie himself to one woman?"

Klews sighed and moved to sit at a chair behind his desk. "That's exactly why I think this is a true mating. Dax would never risk tying himself down to one woman unless it was his true mate. A true mate is someone that the beast inside of us and we ourselves love. Only if both are in agreement can it be a true mate. Normally what happens is the human side falls in love or picks a partner and then their animal grows to accept their choice. With a true mating, there is a bond that isn't there in other pairings. A lot of times it will start with a couple dream sharing, they will be drawn to each other almost uncontrollably, and there will, of course, be an intense desire to have sex and during sex their animal will want to mark the other. Stake their claim I guess. Which is again why I believe that this is a true mating."

"This is just ridiculous! Absurd! Dax does not love me! I don't love him! It was just sex!"

She was screaming at Klews, she knew she sounded desperate, but she couldn't help it. So much was happening in her life the last thing she needed was what Klews was telling her. It was just impossible, there was no way that he could be in love with her. They fought constantly, almost since the moment they'd met, and now she was supposed to believe that he'd fallen for her to the point he would risk his life?

What he was saying explained what she was

feeling, though, what she had felt since she'd met Dax. Her cat had always been interested in him, she'd felt it even before the inhibitor chip was removed, though, she hadn't known what it was, and yes she had thought she was falling in love with him but could she really stay with him for the rest of her life? It was just too soon to make that kind of decision.

Making up her mind she said, "We'll just have to talk to someone when we get to Andove. There has to be a way to stop this. A way that doesn't involve Dax dying."

She took a deep breath to collect herself, she smiled and told Klews good bye, and good luck. Leaving the medical bay she missed Klews shaking his head and chuckling, he knew she didn't stand a chance against Dax.

Chapter Six

The shuttle they were using was small, barely more than a cabin. It had been pieced together by Zeke and while it ran excellently it was not pretty to look at. It was a mismatch of parts, with patches all over the hull. The inside wasn't much better. Since it was used to salvage there was very little in the way of amenities. There was a bed wedged into the back right beside a small closet that contained a toilet, just a small pad to stand on for a sonic shower, and the most basic food receptacle.

When Sasha boarded she stowed her gear in the only overhead bin available and made her way to the front where Dax was seated going through a preflight checklist. He could tell she was nervous, there was also a lot of tension in her face. He fought back the desire to throw her to the cabin floor and mount her, forcing himself to focus on what he was doing and shoving his cat back down. There would be plenty of time to seduce her, he just needed patience. It was hard to be patient though when he found her scent so arousing.

Finishing up the checklist he started the undocking procedure. He could feel her tension escalating and a small scent of fear started coming off of her.

"It's safe."

"What?"

"The shuttle. It's safe. It's small but completely reliable, Zeke wouldn't let us use it if it wasn't. He's a complete fanatic when it comes to safety."

"Right. I'm sure."

She paused and he thought she wasn't going to say anything else, but she surprised him when she said, "I'm still getting used to flying in space. The stars streaming by kind of scare me. The vastness of it all, you know."

"It actually bothers a lot of people. Our minds aren't able to comprehend just how large the universe is and yet we're hurtling through at incredible speeds."

"You aren't helping."

"Sorry. Once I get the coordinates programmed in, and we're on our way, I can turn off the viewer."

Just a few minutes later he did just that and he heard a sigh. The sound brought his attention to her lips. Her full lips. Lips he wanted to ravish and explore with his tongue. When her eyes widened he knew she could smell his arousal. Biting the inside of his cheek, he fought to control himself. He wasn't going to win her with brute force it was going to take patience and finesse. If he played his cards right he could have her mated to him in three days when they landed on Andove. His cat didn't like the idea of waiting, even that long, and a low growl made its way out of his throat before he could stop it.

She cleared her throat at the noise and started talking, "I spoke to Klews before we left. He seemed to think that you had mated yourself to me. He said that's what the bite mark was, but that's silly. You're not the type to settle down to one woman."

Surprised and worried about what else Klews

might have said he started to answer but Sasha was agitated now and jumped up from her seat to begin pacing in the small cabin.

"It's ridiculous to even think about, but Klews seemed positive. He said that since I hadn't bitten you that we weren't fully mated but that if we didn't you could possibly die. I mean there's no way you would take that kind of risk on a woman. I know your type, you would never do something like that, it sounds too permanent. The way he explained it you wouldn't be able to live without me." She snorted at that and stopped her pacing to look at him.

Frowning he wasn't happy with what she was saying.

"You know my type? What exactly do you mean by that?"

Shrugging she said, "Just that you're the kind that love them and leave them. You're all about one-night stands, you don't commit to one woman you leave a string of broken hearts behind you. I saw plenty of guys like you in college."

"Just because I can turn into an animal doesn't make me one. For your information I have never led a woman on, each of my partners knew what they were getting into when we had sex, and they each enjoyed themselves, and I know you did too."

"Exactly! We enjoyed each other now let's move on, there's no need for any kind of lifelong attachment."

"No."

"What do you mean no? There is no, no. This is what you do, we've had sex, we enjoyed ourselves, now it's over and we move on."

He could scent her growing desperation and he

didn't understand it. Why was she so adamant that they be a one night stand? He thought about forcing the issue. He even stood up to face her, arms crossed ready for a battle, but at the last minute he stopped himself. There was obviously something else going on here, something that she wasn't telling him. So he decided to let her cool off before he forced the issue.

Sitting back down and turning to the console he said, "Ok."

"Ok? Ok. Good. I'm glad that's settled."

Sighing she plopped back down in her seat and began fiddling with the screen in front of her until it brought up a book to read and she settled in for a long journey.

Dax fought down a smirk. She had a lot to learn if she thought he was going to give up that easily. A plan began to form in his mind and her belief that things were over would make them that much easier. He couldn't wait to get started.

Just a couple hours later she let out a huge sigh and pushed away from the screen. Getting up she began pacing in the small space. Eventually, she'd had enough and announced that she was going to bed.

"You can take the bed, I'll just sleep in the chair," he said.

Hesitating she almost said something, he could see the words on her lips and he silently begged her to invite him to sleep with her. Instead, she just nodded her head and headed to the back of the ship. A few minutes later she was under the covers and asleep.

Dax opened the view screen and watched as the stars streamed past. He frowned and tried to think of a way to pursue Sasha without her realizing what he was doing. His cat didn't understand why they couldn't just pounce her, but the thought of tricking her into loving them intrigued it. The question was how?

It was obvious that Sasha had been hurt in the past by someone, maybe several someone's, and that she thought he would do the same. He made no apologies for his past, he loved women and loved sleeping with them. He had made a point to never lead any of them on, though, there were a few that tried to get him to stay. He'd always politely declined and kept his distance after that.

Half an hour later, still no closer to a plan, Dax closed the viewer and tried to go to sleep. He slowly slipped into a fitful slumber still trying to discover a way to make the woman he loved fall for him.

Chapter Seven

Running through the tall grass of the savannah she searched for his scent. Finding him was her priority and she looked for hours until a whisper of a breeze brought it to her.

Crouching low she moved like a ghost, hiding her approach until she was right on top of him. Peeking through the grass at the panther stretched out, sunbathing, near the banks of a river she marveled at his glossy black coat.

Digging her claws into the packed earth she prepared to pounce, but she was too late. His seemingly relaxed state was a trick and before she had a chance to react he was on top of her. Rolling in the dirt they bit and clawed each other, never breaking the skin, their attack playful until it became something else.

Aroused Sasha woke up, unsure what she had just been dreaming. All she knew was that she needed Dax. A noise brought her attention to the front of the ship and there he was, hands clenched around the armrests. A vein in his neck bulged and a low growl came from his lips.

"Are you ok?"

She started to get out of bed when he spoke through clenched teeth. "Don't move."

"Why?"

"Just don't. I can smell your arousal and it's taking all that I have not to go over there and taste every inch of you."

She shivered at the thought and her nipples grew hard. Making up her mind in an instant she threw back the covers.

"I'm not going to stop you."

His eyes were intense and he didn't move. He had to make sure she was serious. Once he started he didn't think he'd be able to stop. Her arousal filled the small cabin and intertwined with his own. Their shared dream was the normal first step in the mating dance, but he hadn't thought it would happen since he'd already bitten her. The intimacy from the dream had been nothing he'd ever felt before. Their closeness and the passion their cats felt for each other was intoxicating and it had taken all he could, when the connection broke, not to continue where the dream left off.

Sasha shivered unsure why he wasn't accepting her invitation. Was he over her already? She could see how tense his body was from across the room, he was holding himself back but why? Was he only reacting because of the arousal he smelled, or could he really have feelings for her?

Disappointed when he didn't move to join her, she pulled the covers back up and turned her body away so he couldn't see her fight to control tears. She knew what he had said earlier, but there was a part of her that still hoped he felt something. Now she knew.

Her disappointment gave him the permission he wasn't able to ask for. Moving across the cabin he shed his clothes and then slipped into the bed. He pulled her close and began to nuzzle her neck, inhaling her scent. He felt her tears against his cheek and he gently turned her around so that he could look at her face.

"Why are you crying?"

"I'm not."

Sniffing loudly after her denial ruined the lie. He reached up and softly brushed the tears away. Cupping her cheek, he stared into her eyes. When another tear slowly slipped from her eye he leaned forward and kissed it away.

"Please don't cry. Tell me what I can do."

She sniffed again and then groaned rolling away from him. He propped himself up on his elbow and looked at her as she swung her legs off the bed and rubbed her face.

"I don't know why I'm crying. I don't normally do this, Anika's the weepy one. I'm tough, I don't cry."

Another loud sniff proved her wrong. He moved across the bed and pulled her into his arms. His desire for her was still strong, but his concern overrode it. He felt helpless as she cried into his shoulder no longer trying to hide what she was doing. Great big sobs racked her body as he continued to hold her.

An hour later she was quiet, rolled up into a ball in his arms, asleep. He still had no idea what had caused the tears but holding her in his arms had been an experience he'd never had before. With any other woman he knew he would be afraid of the intensity of the emotion he felt, but with Sasha one look at her tear streaked face and he fell further in love with her.

His arms tightened around her as he moved to lay in the bed. He pulled her close and drifted off to sleep.

Sasha woke up hours later. Disoriented she looked around, remembering where she was slowly, she noticed Dax's arm resting at her waist. Embarrassment flushed her skin as she remembered her break down.

She couldn't recall the last time she'd cried herself to sleep and to do it in front of Dax. She was humiliated. Everything had hit her all at once and as soon as the first tear fell she couldn't stop the rest.

She started to creep out from under his arm and leave the bed but as soon as she moved his arm tightened around her pulling her back against his chest. His warm, solid, bare chest. Her hand reached behind her, moving down his body until she realized.

"You're naked!"

"Yup."

He began to nibble on her neck and a shiver went down her body.

Fighting to keep control she asked, "Why are you naked?"

"Sex is easier naked."

His lips were leaving a trail of fire down her neck. She could feel her nipples pebble under the sheets and a flush was beginning to creep up her body. She knew this was wrong, that it would just cause her feelings to grow, but she couldn't find the will power to stop him.

Moaning, her eyelids closed and her head tilted back, giving him easier access to her vulnerable throat. There was no hesitation as he took her invitation. He flipped her around in one deft movement and his lips claimed hers.

Through resisting Sasha attacked his mouth. Exploring with her tongue and occasionally nipping with her teeth she gave herself over to the burning desire she felt for Dax.

Last night he held her in his arms as she cried and not once did he try and bring things back to sex. Maybe she had judged him too soon. Maybe he wasn't like the other players she knew. Either way she was done thinking and when his hands moved down her body she moved giving him easier access.

Her own hands were roaming across his body, she didn't think she'd get tired of feeling the strength that flowed through his muscles or the light layer of hair that covered his chest. When he cupped her breast she felt a bolt of lightning flash through her body and she jumped. Letting out a giggle she didn't think she'd ever heard come from her lips.

His fingers paused as they played across her nipple and his head pulled back.

"Make that sound again."

She blushed, this time not from passion.

"No."

He growled and dipped his head taking the nipple he'd been tweaking into his mouth. A small bite was enough to send another flash of lightning through her but this time she didn't giggle she moaned and her hand went to the back of his head holding it to her breast.

With his mouth busy his hands began to journey farther down her body. Skimming over her flat stomach to the light thatch of hair between her legs. He began to play with her, just lightly caressing her lips but not quite touching her clit. She shifted her hips trying to get his fingers to connect to her hot button, but he wouldn't let them.

She let out a growl of her own and she felt his lips smile around her nipple right before his fingers began to strum her little nub. His fingers were so quick and sure that within minutes she was on the edge of release. She was sure he was going to stop any minute and she was prepared to kill him if he did, but as the intense feeling of her body reaching peak overwhelmed her all murderous thoughts flew from her mind.

A roar she'd never heard before left her throat and an almost uncontrollable urge to bite and mark him as hers forever flashed through her mind. She resisted long enough for a wave of passion to overcome and wash away the temptation. Before she could regain her balance she felt him move his hand and position himself above her. When he slide inside it was like a part of her that had been missing was coming home.

His slow strokes had her pleasure building back to peak. Her hands went to his back and she dug her heels into his side. She tried to urge him on faster, but he just smiled and continued at his slow pace.

She was so close, again. She writhed under him trying to make him go faster but when he didn't break his pace she chose another tactic. She began to nibble on his earlobe then moved lower to his jaw line. She felt it tense beneath her lips and she smiled and moved lower until her lips were over the very place she wanted to bite.

Licking and nibbling her way across his throat a slight sheen of sweat began to bead on his chest and she knew she was pushing him to his breaking point. He just needed one little push and when her teeth brushed the area that was all he needed.

He slammed into her over and over. The slap of their flesh filled the room and her second orgasm of the night flooded her body. With her mouth right on his neck this time she wasn't able to resist the animal urge and with just the slightest amount of pressure her sharp canine teeth broke the skin and a drop of his blood hit her mouth.

For the second time in her life, she felt a

pleasure so intense, so powerful, that she thought she would die as it filled her body. Another roar left her lips to be joined by the roar that was coming from Dax.

Chapter Eight

She lounged on a rock, basking in the warmth of the sun. Slowly rolling over so that the rays could hit her sensitive stomach. She stretched and as she did a slight breeze brought his scent to her. The scent of her mate.

Contentment was quickly nudged aside by concern over how her human half would react. She'd always been kept bottled inside, never being allowed to act until she couldn't take the chance her human side would let their mate die. She'd fought for control so that she could finish the mating and finally won.

The concern was edged aside by the growing desire for her mate. Even though she'd just had him her need to have him again grew at an uncontrollable pace. This was the beginning of their mating, hopefully, her human half survived it.

Dazed Sasha came back down to earth to feel Dax moving inside of her and she moaned as another orgasm came washing over her.

Still not fully aware she looked up into Dax's face, confused at all the emotions tumbling around inside of her. Looking at him she noticed every crease, every line, every freckle, and she loved all of it. But how? She knew that before she'd had feelings for him, she was pretty sure they were love, but now there was no comparison. She felt like every fiber of her body hummed for him and him alone.

Pushing away from him she shimmied off the bed. Grabbing her clothes she put them on and moved to the front of the ship away from where he was lying naked. She needed to get away from him. She needed to be able to think and with his scent all around her, on her, she couldn't.

He sat up, propping himself on his elbow and looked at her. He'd hoped when she bit him that everything would be ok, but it was obviously not. Watching her panic grow he motioned to the bathroom unit, "Why don't you take a shower?"

Her eyes were wild as she ran for the unit. The door slid shut behind her and he fell back on the bed. How was he going to convince her that what she was feeling was real now? He hadn't planned for this to happen, but her lioness evidently wasn't patient enough for him to act.

Groaning he rubbed his face and tried to come up with ways to salvage the situation. He just needed to reassure her what she was feeling was real and not just a side effect of the mating ritual. That he truly did love her and was more than excited at the prospect of spending the rest of their lives together. That was it. Not going to be difficult at all.

Chapter Nine

Eyes wide with fear Sasha had to fight down a desire to claw at the walls. She felt like she was being smothered, like she had no control over anything that was happening. Blacks dots started dancing in her vision and she sat down on the toilet and dropped her head between her knees. Her normal yoga breathing was doing nothing to control the all-consuming fear she was feeling. She'd lost control of everything and she didn't see when she would ever regain it back.

She was an alien princess that had just completed a mating ritual that bound a man she barely knew to her for life. How had this happened in the span of a few days?

She tried to talk herself down but saying everything was going to be okay when she knew full well it wouldn't was not helping. In fact, things were starting to get worse. Her breathing was too fast and she started to slide from the toilet as she began to pass out.

A swirling mist surrounded her and Sasha lost complete control as her lioness took over for the first time. Her body reformed and sharp shoots of pain shot down every limb like they had fallen asleep and were being awakened after a long time. When the mist cleared the too small space was filled with a large powerful cat. Her heavyweight against the door of the bathroom was too much and it burst open causing her to fall on the bed.

"What the hell?"

Leaping out of the way in time to avoid being crushed Dax looked down at the most beautiful lioness he'd ever seen. Her golden fur was like warm sand and her eyes like melted gold. He was floored over how gorgeous she was and fell to his knees taking in every change of color in her coat and how even the artificial light in the room couldn't dull the gleam coming from her sleek fur.

"So beautiful."

Sasha's lioness ignored him as she stretched out to her full length on the bed. He felt a thread of pleasure from their freshly created mating bond and he knew that she appreciated the comment. As she got comfortable Dax continued to marvel at her size and how graceful she was.

Shifters were larger than the earth animals he'd seen, but the royal families were supposed to be larger than even regular shifters. He was getting to see firsthand that it was definitely true in Sasha's case. She took up every inch of the queen size bed with her tail and parts of her paws falling off the side.

"So are you enjoying being free?"

Her purr caused the floor beneath his feet to vibrate even more than it already was from the engines. The warm sound filled the cabin and a smile split his face. Dax tried to find a place on the bed to sit, but there wasn't even an inch available for him. The cabin was barely big enough for two humans and definitely wasn't big enough for a shifted Andovian.

"Darling you're amazing, but I think it might be time to shift back. There's no room and I really need to talk to Sasha."

The purring stopped and her golden eyes met his. Through their mating bond, he could clearly tell that she had no intention of changing back anytime soon.

"I know she kept you locked in there for a long time, but beautiful, Sasha and I need to get things settled before we get to Andove."

He reached out to gently rub the fur behind her ears, but her lip curled back and she snapped her massive jaws at him. Barely pulling his hand back in time he frowned at her.

"What was that for?"

She growled and stood up in the bed. Her back hit the ceiling as she circled the bed, trying to get comfortable, until she settled herself. She rested her head on her paws and then closed her eyes. A few minutes later soft snores started coming from her and Dax realized she had fallen asleep.

"What the hell am I supposed to do?"

Chapter Ten

Two days later they were just a few hours from Andove and Sasha was still in lioness form. Dax was furious. He'd tried coaxing, bribing, even threatening, but her lioness refused to give back control. Klews had warned Sasha that this could happen if she kept denying that side of her, but Dax never believed she would get in the way of their mating heat.

He was bouncing off the walls with sexual frustration. At first it had been muted, having sex in animal form was not done, but as the hours passed his newly created mating bond kept reminding him that he should be making long sweet love. Her lioness clearly wasn't feeling the same way.

Staring at the console he watched as they came closer to Andove and he knew once they arrived there would be no time for what he desperately needed to do. Standing up he walked back to the bed and growled at her.

Lifting her large head from her paws Sasha's lioness met his stare without blinking.

"Listen to me you spoiled brat. We're going to be arriving soon and if I don't get a chance to talk to Sasha all that happens afterward is going to be your fault. Do you think she's going to like meeting her family for the first time with no prep what so ever? Do you think she's going to be eager to let you take control again?"

The lioness blinked and then let out a huge yawn, making sure that Dax saw each of her long sharp teeth. He roared and walked back to the front of the ship before he lost control and did something he would regret.

A sound caused him to turn around just as the mists of change receded and Sasha stood in front of him. Naked. She wobbled when she took her first few steps from the bed, but she was running by the time she hit him. Her lips were on his devouring him. Her hands were shaking as they ripped his shirt from his torso, shredding it with her strength.

When her hands made contact with his skin his control snapped. After two days denying the mating heat, they both were giant bottles of need and it was going to be a miracle if they made it through the next few hours alive. Their hands were everywhere, desperately touching every inch they could access.

Dax tried to take her back to the bed, but Sasha wouldn't let him and instead pushed him back into the captain's seat. Her hands reached around his waist and once again she didn't have the control to wait and just ripped his pants off of him in strips. When his cock sprung free, his erection was so hard it was almost too painful. A sharp gasp escaped his lips and was quickly swallowed by Sasha.

Her lips parted and her tongue darted into his mouth as their kiss deepened. While her mouth was occupied Sasha straddled Dax and without any preamble plunged herself down onto his thick sword. Their heads fell back and roars of pleasure filled the room. His hands moved to her waist as she started working herself up and down his cock. Her pace was frenzied and it took all of Dax's control to stop himself from adding to the pace.

As her first orgasm started rolling through her body and her pace slowed, only slightly, Dax lost his control and started thrusting into her with all the desperation he had been fighting the last two days. Seconds after he emptied his load into her he was ready to go again. Standing up he took Sasha to the bed and placed her down on the edge, never once leaving the sheath of her body.

Over and over he thrust into her, losing track of the number of times they both came. There was no finesse, no romance, they were victims of the mating heat that had been denied for too long. At some point during the marathon session, Dax had the forethought to slow the ship down and give them more time before arriving on Andove.

Five hours later the heat was finally cooling down. The desire was still there, but they were able to resist it. Sweaty and exhausted they lay beside each other in bed staring up at the ceiling.

Groaning Sasha said, "I feel so sore."

"A quick change into your lioness would fix that and any other minor injuries you may have."

"Yeah I don't think so, what if she won't let me back out?"

He propped himself up on his elbow so that he could look down at her. "I don't think she'll do that again." Clearly not believing him Sasha just shook her head. He started tracing lines on her bare skin and he smiled when he saw the goose bumps raised on her flat stomach. He bent down and started placing gentle kisses on her skin. The fire between her legs that she had finally thought was extinguished rushed to life and she needed to feel him again.

Pushing him over onto his back Sasha straddled him and when she leaned over her bare breasts brushed his chest. Her lips claimed his in a mind-searing kiss that shouldn't have been possible after all this time. Tearing herself away she shimmied her way down his body until her mouth was hovering over his stiff member.

Wrapping her hand around the base she squeezed tightly enjoying the warm hard length of him. Her head dipped down, her lips parted, and she took him deep into her mouth. Her tongue swirled around as she began gently sucking. His gasp let her know she was on the right track.

Working up and down his shaft, taking him in deeply, she found the perfect rhythm for her mouth and hand working on his cock in tandem. The heat between her thighs started to pool as she lost herself in the feel of his hard silkiness between her lips. He let lose a sexy growl and a smile curved hers at the noise.

As her free hand began to sneak between her thighs to relieve the ache building there, Dax sat up and lifted her body up. Laying back down he placed her hot pussy over his mouth and left her facing his considerably aroused staff. As his tongue started stroking her clit she lowered her head back down and took him back in her mouth. Her pace had renewed vigor as he continued to use his tongue to bring her closer and closer to release.

Her body reached its peak and just one more push would be enough to shatter her world. As she squeezed his cock tight between her hands and bobbed down, his tongue thrust into her starting the chain reaction of her orgasm. Her scream was muffled by his cock as she began frantically gobbling him up until she tasted the creamy saltiness of his cum in her mouth.

When she was finished slowly licking the cum off of his deflating member she rolled off of him and lay on her back looking up at the ceiling.

"That's it. I don't think I'll ever orgasm again. Seriously. I've lost count. I have no idea how many times I've cum in the last six hours, but it has the be a record."

Chuckling Dax propped himself up on his elbow. When he reached out to trace a bead of sweat between her breasts she slapped his hand away.

"Stop it."

"Never."

That was the wrong thing to say. As soon as the word left his lips Dax saw the concern fill Sasha's eyes. He could actually see when her brain kicked in and she started thinking about everything her sex starved mind had pushed to the back of her brain. When she got out of the bed, she gathered her clothes, and quietly closed the door to the bathroom, he put his arm over his eyes and groaned. When the alarm sounded letting him know they'd arrived at their destination he knew things were about to get even more complicated.

Chapter Eleven

Staring at her reflection in the small square mirror above the toilet Sasha tried to figure out what had happened to her life. She'd taken a sonic shower so Dax's scent was no longer clinging to every inch of her skin, but that just made things worse. She wanted his scent. She wanted people to know that she was his and that he was most definitely hers. Did she want all of that because of a bite though? Because he was supposedly her true mate? What did that even mean?

Closing her eyes, she took a deep breath and began pushing all of those feelings and thoughts to the back of her brain. They were life changing thoughts, but she had more pressing matters. They had landed on the surface of Andove and the Royal Guard were on their way to escort her to the palace.

When she finished her shower she'd poked her head out of the room to ask if Dax wanted to clean up, but he'd already been dressed and in the captain's chair. He declined, and she knew it was because he preferred to have her scent on him. Should she not have showered? Did she hurt his feelings when she did?

There was so much she didn't know. Clenching her teeth she tried to bring her line of thought back to the upcoming meeting with her family. The closest she'd ever been to royalty was watching movies about princesses when she was a little girl. All the fancy clothes and rules never appealed to her so she hadn't paid attention to the royalty back on Earth.

Clothes. Her face white she looked down at the black pantsuit she was wearing. Princesses wore dresses and designer clothes. Her clothes came from a big box department store. She'd been a lawyer for less than a year and worked in a small city, her income hadn't had a chance to trickle down to nicer clothes. The trim dark pantsuit was the nicest thing she owned, but only because she'd splurged on the white silk sleeveless shirt underneath. What kind of impression did it make for the royal family to see her wearing business clothes?

A gentle tap at the door let her know Dax was waiting for her. Shoulders slumped she left the safety of the bathroom and moved closer to the unknown. Dax tried to cheer her up. With his big grin and self-deprecating humor she should have at the very least been able to join in and make jokes at his expense, but she couldn't move past what was about to happen.

Silence filled the cabin when he realized her mood wasn't going to be changed. The viewer was open to the empty runway in front of them. With each passing minute, Sasha grew more anxious until the small space was filled with the scent of her nerves. Unable to take it anymore Dax stood up and pulled her into his arms. Cradling her against his hard body he made soothing sounds.

"Everything is going to be okay. They aren't going to eat you. They've been searching for you for years."

She felt like she should be crying, she was terrified, but that side of her had shut down. It was like when she met new foster parents. When she was younger she'd always been hopeful, maybe these people would be her forever parents, but after several failed placements she lost hope. Each time she met a new family her emotions shut down and she waited for them to send her away and each time they did. Would her own family send her away?

"Sasha talk to me. What are you thinking?"

Concerned at the cold that was coming from Sasha's body Dax rubbed his hands up and down her back, pulling her in closer, but the longer he held her the colder she grew. The nervousness that had filled his nose earlier causing him such concern was gone and all that was left was a chilly frost. The only time he'd ever felt anything remotely like this was in the military when he met a sniper about to leave on assignment.

Pulling out of his arms Sasha adjusted her sleeves as she answered, "I'm fine. I just wish we could get this over with so that we can get back to the others and find Kelly. Maybe we could get help while we're here and then the whole trip won't be a total waste."

"What? Are you serious? Your family isn't just going to let you leave after twenty years of not knowing where you were."

She shrugged her shoulders, clearly not believing they would care what she did. He frowned and tried to figure out why she was acting this way. There was nothing coming through on the mating bond they shared, so he had no clue where these new emotions were coming from. When they were on the ship she'd never seemed indifferent to the fact she was a princess, more like terrified, and now she was acting like it was no big deal. She was just going to pop in say hello and then continue on with your life.

"Sasha, I don't think things are going to go how you expect them too. These people have been searching the universe for you, for a very long time."

She cut him off, "I don't want to talk about. Let's just go outside and wait for them in the fresh air. Please."

Wanting to push the issue he opened his mouth to argue but when she tilted her chin up and narrowed her eyes he knew it was a lost cause. A few keystrokes later the departure ramp was lowering and they walked out into the clean fresh air of Andove. Tilting his head up, Dax closed his eyes as the sun beat down on his face.

Home. It had been so long, too long. After breathing the recycled air of the ship and before that the polluted air of Earth, being on Andove was a stark difference. Looking at Sasha he could tell she'd never tasted air so pure before. Her face had gone pink and she was taking tiny little sips like she was savoring it.

"Beautiful, isn't it?"

She could only nod. This was incredible. They were on a runway in what looked like a very busy airport, the air shouldn't taste this amazing. Her eyes started to tear up and black spots danced in her vision. Dax was by her side instantly, wrapping his arm around her.

"Breathe woman. You've got to breath."

On the verge of passing out she took a deep breath and her lungs rejoiced. She'd been on a new planet for less than five minutes and almost killed herself. She was going to be great at her new intergalactic life.

Blushing she pushed Dax's arms away, "I'm fine. It's just weird being on a new planet. The air tastes different and I swear the gravity is different."

Putting his hands in his pockets Dax smiled as Sasha started skipping around the shuttle. "Actually the gravity is the same as on Earth. The air is cleaner, your lungs are probably getting to breath well for the first time in years."

She laughed at him, "You aren't happy to be home at all, are you?"

Dax smiled at her laughter, he'd been concerned earlier, but it looked like she was going to be alright. He started to make plans for their stay on Andove, momentarily forgetting why they were there when a transport pulled up and out stepped ambassador Ariel Levon and her entourage.

Ariel was Sasha's aunt, but before he could mention that, Ariel had marched across the runway and was sizing Sasha up.

"Well you certainly look like a Levon, but then they always do. Appearances are the easiest to change."

Holding her hand out one of the entourage placed a device in it. Stepping forward Ariel grabbed Sasha's arm and pressed the device to it, drawing some blood. Jumping back Sasha yelped and rubbed her arm. Dax strode forward putting himself between the two women.

"What the hell was that?"

Sneering at him, Ariel handed the sample to a member of her party who immediately walked to a porting platform on the side of the runway and ported away.

"You didn't actually think we would take your word that this is the lost princess. Do you have any idea how many imposters there are each year?"

Dax snarled at her, "If you think she's an

imposter why are you here? Why not some lackey? Why would they send her aunt?"

"I vet every claim to the title. It is my responsibility as an ambassador as well as my duty as family. We would never leave something this important to anyone but family." She looked down her nose at Dax, exuding an air of superiority and distaste for his prescience.

Their glaring match was interrupted by Sasha's soft voice, "You're my aunt?"

Dax immediately went to her side, "I wanted to tell you before she arrived, but there wasn't time."

Shaking her head Sasha reassured him, "It was just a shock I wasn't expecting to meet family so quickly. I thought I would have to go through security or something, I don't know. I just didn't think... my aunt. I had no idea."

Tears started to pool in Sasha's eyes and she blushed, she hated showing any kind of weakness, and despite her recent breakdowns she rarely cried. When she saw her aunt roll her eyes in obvious disdain her tears dried up instantly. She wasn't sure what she wanted more, to prove Ariel wrong or be proven wrong. It would certainly solve a lot of problems if she turned out not to be the princess.

"Let's get this show on the road. I assume that wasn't the last test?"

A smirk crossed Ariel's lips when she replied, "Oh my dear, that was just the beginning."

Chapter Twelve

The tests ran for forty-eight hours. Porting from the airport directly to a sterile lab she'd been stripped of her clothes and every possible fluid imaginable had been taken from her. Once that was done they'd given her puke green scrubs to wear and placed her in a small, white room. There was a table in the center with chairs on either side. Scattered glowing tiles in the ceiling were the only source of light.

A man in a white lab coat walked into the room, sat in the chair opposite her and started asking her a never ending list of questions, ranging from when she'd gotten her first period to what her favorite color was. During that time, Sasha didn't sleep and was given no food. As the questions continued on she grew angrier and angrier. The more volatile her emotions grew the harder it was to control her lioness.

When the questions ended they led her to a gym where Dax was waiting for her. He rushed to her side, "Are you okay? They wouldn't tell me what was going on or where you were."

She hugged him tight. All too soon she had to pull out of his arms. "I'm okay. Hungry and tired, but I'll live. They were just asking me questions. A billion questions, no joke, I counted."

He pulled her back into his arms and breathed a

silent sigh of relief. Their mating heat was still strong and it had been two days since he'd seen her last. His panther had been going wild inside of him and if she had been kept from him another minute he would have torn the place apart. Only his military training had given him the ability to resist the urge for so long.

A lab tech walked in and frowned when he saw the two of them embracing. His nostrils flared and his eyes grew wide before he hurried away. Dax's eyes narrowed, it looked like their secret had gotten out. No Andovian could mistake the scent in the air, the scent of a couple in the middle of the mating dance.

The doctor running all of Sasha's tests walked in minutes later followed by a group of armed guards. Sasha's lioness was barely back under control, but she nearly lost it when they escorted Dax away.

As more lab techs filed in she could hear them whispering among themselves, "I heard he was in the military."

"I heard he was dishonorably discharged."

She growled, how dare they make comments about Dax, they had no idea who he was or what he'd been through. Her eyes glowed gold and she could feel her claws beginning to sharpen.

"Sasha that's enough."

Turning from the frightened techs she met the gaze of her aunt. She swallowed down a roar and pushed her lioness back down. In control again she asked, "Are my tests done? It's been two days now, surely everything has come back. Am I the lost princess or not?"

Ariel wouldn't meet her eyes as she walked around the room. "The tests have been...inconclusive."

"Inconclusive? What the hell does that mean?"

"It means we run more tests."

Sasha snarled at that, of course, there were more. It's not like she'd answered enough questions already. How much longer was this going to take? Could she just give up and leave? Actually that was a good question, was she a prisoner or could she leave. Before she could ask her aunt met the gaze of her doctor, nodded, and then left the room. What was that about?

"All right Sasha, your next round of tests are about to begin. Now we'll be testing your physical health, your reflexes, and stamina, along with a few other things."

He gestured to the treadmill in the middle of the room. Gritting her teeth, Sasha decided if they didn't at least feed her soon she was going to show him how fast her reflexes were.

Chapter Thirteen

Watching Sasha through the surveillance system in the adjoining room Dax had to bite back a growl. This was not what he'd expected when he brought her home. They'd run too many tests, something wasn't right. He paced in the small room. There was a heavily armed guard on the door which was the only thing keeping him from leaving and taking Sasha with him.

She was running, flat out, on the treadmill. Each of the techs were monitoring their screens making notes and adjustments, but the doctor, he was just staring at her. He knew what was going on. He knew that Sasha was the princess, but why hadn't he stopped the tests?

The door to his little prison opened and the distinctive odor of Ariel Levon met his nose. He refused to turn around and face her, breaking all the rules of protocol he'd learned while in the service, instead he kept his eyes on Sasha. She was all that mattered. He could smell Ariel's anger at the insult and his lips quirked up.

"Soldier you will face me now or I will have you beaten."

He paused, letting her know that he was turning because he wanted to, not because she was ordering him. Her lips were raised showing her sharpened canines, he smiled at her obvious anger. Pissing off Levon women was becoming his specialty.

"Sit."

He rolled his eyes but didn't push it this time. Glaring at him she took a deep breath to bring her anger back under control. The scent of her ire disappeared and she sat down across from him. Glancing over his shoulder to the image of Sasha Ariel's brow furrowed.

"She doesn't remember anything, does she?"

"Nope."

Her eyes narrowed and met his, clearly he needed to work on his tone. "Why is that?"

He shrugged his shoulders, "There's a reason inhibitor chips are banned on Andove. I'm sure your medical scans can still detect a residue left by it."

Nodding she looked over his shoulder again toward Sasha, "You didn't waste any time mating her."

It was his turn to frown, "She's my true mate. My panther saw her and claimed her when my control slipped."

Ariel's breathing changed and when she leaned forward the movement was barely perceptible, her words came out just above a whisper, "Has she claimed you?"

He pulled the collar of his shirt down to show the still red mark. His chest puffed out in pride, he was Sasha's and no one could change that.

A small sigh escaped from Ariel's lips and she leaned back. Her frown was back and Dax had to fight the urge to say face was going to stick that way if she kept it up. It was probably too late for that anyway.

"You've complicated matters, Dax."

He leaned back, matching her relaxed pose, "Really? That's not how I see it. I've just returned the long-lost princess of the Feline Royal Family. Shouldn't I be getting a medal or something?"

Snapping her fingers, an aid hurriedly entered the room and placed a tablet in her outstretched hand. The aid disappeared while Ariel began tapping on the surface of the device. Turning it around to him he could see that she had pulled up his military file. There was a line of red text at the top that stated he was dishonorably discharged. When he'd found out who Sasha was his first thought had been that she could fix what had happened to him, but when he'd discovered she was his mate those thoughts had fled. She was all that he cared about, it stung to see those words by his name, but they no longer mattered. All that mattered was Sasha.

"Am I supposed to be impressed? What does my military record have to do with anything?"

A small growl came from across the table and a smile quirked his lips, he loved throwing a wrench in someone's plans. Clearly he was supposed to react a different way, but why? Ariel was a puzzle, there was something else going on here. She knew that Sasha was the princess but was still forcing her to do more tests, now she was waving his record in front of him. What did she want? More importantly was Sasha in danger? His brow furrowed and he tried to spot the threat before it was too late.

Standing up Ariel looked down at him, he knew that she couldn't scent his fear, he was a professional, but he should probably pay attention to what she was saying.

"You're not at all what I expected Dax. When

you contacted us saying you found the princess I glanced at your record. When you arrived I fully expected her to be a fraud and you to be looking for the reward. As soon as I realized that was not the case I reread your file. You were such a promising candidate. Some of your superiors were already discussing giving you a command, then you were court-martialed, and you haven't been planetside since."

Biting the inside of his cheek, he fought back the urge to growl. Lies, it was all lies. He'd been framed, but no one had believed him, and why should they? He was an orphan with no family to stand behind him and declare his innocence. He had been chosen well as a patsy. As much as he wanted to defend his innocence and demand they look into it further, he knew that was exactly what she wanted him to do. He didn't know what was going on, but everything inside of him told him that Ariel was not to be trusted, and the last thing you showed your enemy is what you cared about.

"Hmmm. I guess I judged you wrong again Dax. I promise I won't do that a third time. Before we continue…What is…"

Cutting herself off mid-sentence she rushed from the room. Glancing over his shoulder he saw what had caused the interruption. It looked like Sasha was meeting another family member. Smiling to himself he watched Ariel's plan be destroyed as Princess Laini clung to her sister and cried tears of joy.

Chapter Fourteen

Shocked Sasha looked down at the young woman that was clinging to her. The sound of laughter and crying filled the room and it was all coming from this petite woman. The lab techs heads were lowered and the doctor was staring at the doorway where Ariel was standing frowning at the scene.

Turning away from Sasha, though not letting her go, the young woman said, "Aunt Ariel it's true. I couldn't bring myself to hope, but I overheard someone saying that she had been found."

Smiling up at Sasha she continued, "As soon as I saw her I began to hope but when my lioness caught her scent I knew. This is my sister. After all these years, it's a miracle."

Laughing again she hugged Sasha tight, she was surprisingly strong for someone so tiny. Catching movement out of the corner of her eye Sasha saw Dax enter the room, she silently begged him for help, but he just smiled and shook his head. Of course, he wouldn't save her from this tiny vice crushing the air from her lungs.

Finally unable to take it anymore she started prying herself free. Surprised the young woman looked hurt, which made Sasha feel bad, but she had no idea who this person was and needed some answers.

Actually coming to her aid Ariel began speaking, "Laini, I wish you had come to me first. Things are complicated."

Shaking her head in denial Laini said, "All that matters is that this is my sister. She's returned to us, alive."

Her eyes were shining with tears as she looked up at Sasha who couldn't believe that she had a sister. A sister that didn't even come to her chin.

"Laini, there was an inhibitor chip used and Akali remembers nothing of her family. I've been running tests to see if the effects can be reversed, but so far that doesn't seem possible."

She was lying, Sasha had no idea how she knew that, but through the fog of confusion that was descending on her that was the one thing she knew for certain. Why was she lying? And who was Akali? Was that her real name? Searching for Dax she reached out for him and he came instantly, pulling her into the safety of his arms. She breathed deep, inhaling his scent and drawing strength from him.

Closing her eyes, she leaned into him and blocked out all the confusion that was going on around them. She ignored the lab techs as they filed out of the room and snuggled in closer when the doctor started talking about her medical results. If she ignored it everyone would go away and she could go back to the life she understood. As soon as the thought entered her mind she knew that she had to come back to reality. She never hid from her responsibilities, but she was grateful to Dax for giving her that moment of calm.

Standing on her tiptoes her lips met his in what was supposed to be a quick peck but quickly deepened.

Their newly formed mating bond did not like being denied and it had been days since they'd been given an opportunity to bask in each other.

Moaning she pulled away from Dax. His lips were so distracting that she had almost forgotten their audience. An audience that had shrunk to two people, Ariel and Laini. Ariel's face betrayed nothing, but Laini was as easy to read as a book.

"You found your mate. That's so beautiful. Oh, this is just so splendid. We have to go see Mum and Dad."

Walking forward she grabbed Sasha's hand and then Dax's and began dragging them away. Giggling like a school girl she said, "They're going to be so surprised. We didn't even know that Auntie was evaluating someone."

Sasha's eyes narrowed when she caught Ariel staring at her, there was something going on there and Sasha was starting to think it was a bigger miracle than Laini realized that she'd been found.

Walking through hallway after hallway, Laini chatted non-stop, barely letting up long enough to breath.

"Our parents are going to be overjoyed. We've searched for you since I was a little girl. We've had so many women show up claiming to be you, but they never are. To make matters worse, we've never been able to even figure out how you were kidnaped. Amiri is going to be so happy you've been found. He thinks he's responsible for you being stolen. He hates it when you're brought up because it's the one time he didn't succeed at something. I shouldn't have said that, he's an amazing brother, it's just hard when your oldest brother is perfect and your older sister was kidnaped."

She stopped and turned to Sasha eyes wide, "I didn't mean it like that. I'm sure you had it much worse than me. I wasn't complaining, not really, I've had a very privileged life, except that I can't go anywhere without a full guard, but that's not your fault. Our parents just worry, because that's what parents do, and I am grateful for the fact that I have a loving family and…"

Sasha cut her off, "I understand what you meant. It's okay, you don't have to explain."

Sighing Laini picked up where she'd left off, "I have to take you to our parents immediately."

Panicked Sasha tried to think of something to put off that meeting. When she'd been a child, trapped in horrible foster homes, she'd dreamed of finding her real family, her real parents. Now faced with that finally coming true she was terrified. She shot a pleading look to Dax who just shrugged his shoulders. Grasping at straws she asked, "Could I get something to eat first? I haven't eaten in two days and I'm really hungry."

"You haven't eaten in two days? How is that possible? I'll have to talk to Doctor Williams, that shouldn't have happened. I'm sure Aunt Ariel didn't know or she would have taken care of you."

Shaking her head, Laini changed direction and dragged them behind her. Not once in the entire trip, even when they used a porter, did Laini let go of Sasha's hand. It reminded her of a little girl that had followed her around everywhere at one of her homes. It didn't matter what Sasha was doing she had been there watching and trying to join in. That was the last time Sasha cried when she left a foster home. She'd forgotten about that.

Gripping Laini's hand tighter she was rewarded

with a smile. Maybe having a sister that wouldn't shut up wasn't so bad. A small ounce of happiness began to poke through her armor of cynicism. The minute she'd found out she was a princess, well a few hours later when she'd started to be able to think again, she'd begun making assumptions about her royal family. It looked like at least one expectation was turning out to be false.

Entering a huge kitchen Sasha was met with unfamiliar smells that were intoxicating. Her mouth began to water and her stomach growled so loudly she blushed and hoped no one heard. When Laini squeezed her hand tight she knew she had no such luck.

"Sit down and I'll bring you something. Dax are you hungry?"

He winked and gave her a wicked smile, "I can always eat something."

She giggled and walked away. Sasha jabbed him in the stomach, "What was that? I thought I was the only woman for you now."

He pulled her into his arms and nuzzled her neck causing her nipples to pebble under the scrubs she was wearing. "You are the only one for me, but I can still tease pretty girls that know I'm taken and not being serious."

She shook her head and rolled her eyes. It was unrealistic to think someone like Dax would stop flirting, and as long as he didn't act on it, she didn't have a problem with it. Now if she could just get him to bring his mouth lower and maybe get his hands in on the action. Her mind clouded with lust she forgot where they were and the mating heat started to take over.

A throat clearing was enough to bring her out

of the momentary haze and remind her where she was and that making out with Dax was going to have to wait, though, hopefully not for much longer. It had been way too long since she'd felt him moving inside of her. The image was enough to cause her to get wet and the scent of her arousal filled the air around her.

A scarlet blush crept up her cheeks when she realized that everyone could tell that she was horny. "I'm sorry. I wasn't thinking."

A loud, gruff laugh interrupted her, "Girl we all know what it's like to be in the middle of a mating. Don't worry about it, eat what I give you and you'll have all the strength you need to attack that young man and make him too tired to think let alone flirt with every pretty little thing that walks by."

The woman behind the laugh and words of wisdom towered over her, easily well over six feet, and she had the darkest skin Sasha had ever seen. It was like glossy onyx. The woman's bright blue eyes missed nothing and twinkled at Sasha's embarrassment.

"I didn't realize the Feline royal family was employing bears now. When did that happen?"

Snorting at Dax the woman responded, "When their taste buds woke up and realized that the best chefs have always, and will always, be bears."

Laini stepped out from behind the woman to make introductions, "Sasha this is Chef Yolanda, and she's the best chef on the entire planet. I'm not exaggerating at all, she won Andovian Chef five years in a row before she retired from the competition to take over our kitchens. It's been incredible. Of course, Chef Louis was excellent in his own right, but Yo is simply the best and everything she makes is an unparalleled experience."

"Someone's trying to butter up the chef." The words were out before Sasha even realized it. Laini was clearly offended and started to sputter out a denial when Yo interrupted her with another full-bodied laugh.

"She's teasing you child. It's what normal siblings do, something you missed out on with your stick up the butt brother."

Smiling tentatively Laini tried to recover her compose and asked Sasha, "What would you like to eat? Yo can fix anything and it will be the best you've ever had."

Feeling bad for embarrassing her sister Sasha tried to think of something easy to ask for, but she didn't know any of the food that was around her. "Pizza?"

Shaking his head Dax answered, "There is no pizza on Andove."

"Are you serious? How can you have a civilized society without pizza? We're definitely going to have to fix that and soon." Seeing Laini biting her lip and look worried Sasha hurried on, "I'll eat whatever you have. I'm that hungry it doesn't matter, everything smells amazing."

As if by magic a hot bowl of soup was placed in front of her. Bending over to smell it she detected a few spices that seemed familiar. Taking the spoon offered to her Sasha took a hesitant spoonful and then didn't lift her head up until the bowl was empty. Debating whether or not it would be polite to lick the remaining drops up she was startled out of her food-induced trance by Yo's booming laugh. She was really starting to love that sound. It was all warm and fuzzy and filled her bones with contentment.

"Girl you know how to eat. I'm going to like you. When you've got some free time I'd love to hear more about the food from the planet you've been on, especially pizza."

"Yo if the pizza you make is half as good as that soup I will be forever at your service."

"Who's kissing up now?"

Surprised Sasha looked at her sister and then laughed. Looking proud of herself Laini grabbed her hand and started dragging her from the room while Dax followed behind. It looked like Sasha had stalled as long as she could and it was time to meet her parents.

Chapter Fifteen

Watching Sasha as she grew more nervous the closer they got to her parents, Dax tried to think of something to make her feel better. Taking her free hand, he gave it a slight squeeze to let her know that she wasn't alone. The look of thanks she gave him was enough to settle his panther.

They came to a large ornate double door, Laini didn't even pause as she pushed it open, pulling them into the room. It was surprisingly small, though, the vaulted ceilings made it feel larger than it was. One wall was made up entirely of a force field meant to provide protection but still allow a beautiful view of Galia, the capital city. In the center of the room was a collection of chairs, this must be the personal sitting room of the royal family.

Anxious Dax swallowed a sudden excess of saliva and tried to keep his emotions under control. When he first found out who Sasha was, this was the moment he'd dreamed about. Meeting the royal family and getting them to clear his name. Things hadn't happened exactly the way he'd thought they would, but a small part of him couldn't help but hope it would happen.

"Mother, father, I have big news."

Not even glancing up from her tablet the older woman lounging on a plush couch in the center of the room said, "Laini, sweetheart, you know you're not supposed to barge into rooms."

"But mother this is important. They found Akali. She's here!"

Her voice rose at the end of the sentence until she was screaming and jumping up and down. Sasha's mother looked up sharply and her hand flew to her throat in shock. There was a sharp retort from the other side of the room and Dax cursed himself for missing the king standing there. Bowing immediately Dax was ignored as the king rushed forward.

"Are you sure? How is this possible?"

The queen was shaking as she stood up. "Her eyes Afua. She has your eyes." Stumbling forward she grabbed Sasha's arms and pulled her into a tight embrace. Sobs shook her body and she leaned back into her husband as he came up behind them and surrounded them with his arms.

Laini stood back, hands covering her mouth, as tears streamed down her face. Standing up Dax watched the family tableau unfold and felt like he was intruding, he started to edge his way out of the room when Sasha's hand snaked out and grabbed him. Laini stepped forward into the big group hug and pulled him along with her.

New levels of discomfort were reached in those few minutes while everyone was hugging and most people were crying. When it finally broke up Sasha was led to one of the larger couches in the room and her parents sat her down between them while Laini dragged him to one of the flanking chairs.

"I apologize Dax for being so rude and not

introducing you to begin with, but we've missed Akali for so many years."

"Don't worry about is Princess." Shit was he supposed to call her princess or should he have said your royal highness? The kings head swiveled around to meet him. Frowning he stood up and moved to stand between Sasha and Dax. Not the best thing to do during a mating. Dax's panther immediately went on edge and Dax stood up, his hands clenched at his side.

Moving between the two angry males Laini put her hands up and glared at each of them. "Father this is Dax, he's Akali's mate, he is also the one that found Akali." She stressed the word found and her pointed stare put the king in his place.

Amazed that this slip of a woman could put a man in his place who was known the world over for growing so enraged at an enemy that he literally ripped the man's head from his shoulders, Dax found new respect for Laini. Still the last thing he wanted to do was offend his king and the father of his love. Bowing his head slightly Dax said, "I'm glad that I was able to find and return Sasha to her family, but I am even more grateful to you, my king and queen, for giving me such a wonderful mate."

It was a normal remark to give your new mates parents, well the not the first part, but it seemed to make matters worse and Dax couldn't understand why. Looking to Sasha for help he realized that she was in a state of deep shock. Her eyes were unseeing and she hadn't moved an inch once her parents had pulled her to the couch. Her hand was resting in a position that had to be uncomfortable.

Dropping down in front of her Dax took her hand in his and tried to coax a reaction from her,

"Sasha, are you okay? Can you hear me?"

His hand cupped her cheek and he tried to meet her eyes. She was cold and clammy when the golden gaze of her lioness peeked out he knew she was too far gone and moved away as the mists of change surrounded her. The queen moved away as well, leaving her alone on the couch.

Sasha's lioness took up the entire seat, her tail flicked as she preened under the attention everyone was giving her. Dax was again struck by how large and beautiful she was but was concerned that she wouldn't give control back to Sasha like she had last time.

Standing up the lioness stretched before jumping down and bumping her head against Dax reassuring him that she wouldn't keep control for too long. She sat back down on her haunches and studied her family who hadn't spoken a word since her change.

"Well there's really no question she's ours now, is there?" The queen sounded amused when she spoke. Her hand was holding the kings as he continued to frown at Dax. He wasn't sure if it was because he was mated to his daughter or if it was something else. Andovian males were known to be very protective of their daughters, though, that tended to be a trait mainly held by the Ursa clans. Hopefully once, Sasha changed back she could start convincing her father that Dax wasn't such a bad guy.

"Who are you exactly? Apart from supposedly being my daughter's mate."

Evidently he wasn't going to waste any time. "My names Dax, I'm formally from the FRM (Feline Royal Military), I've spent the last few years working salvage on a ship that myself and two friends own. That's actually how we found Sasha, err, Akali, err,

Princess Akali."

Stopping before he said anything else damaging Dax waited impatiently for what the king would say next. His frown had lessened when Dax told him he had been in the military, though, Dax was sure if he knew he'd been dishonorably discharged that would have made things worse. The king looked more uncertain now, more than anything, he looked shell shocked.

Queen Layla, on the other hand, was glowing. She had one arm wrapped around Laini, with her other she held onto King Afua's hand, and she gazed lovingly at the daughter she hadn't seen in over twenty years. The scent of her love and contentment filled the room and served to further remove the frown from King Afua's face. It also appeared to be calming Sasha because once again the mist of change surrounded her and when they receded she stood before them naked.

Her face beet red Sasha tried to cover herself. After living most of her life on Earth, she wasn't as comfortable as everyone else on Andove was with nakedness. Quickly taking off his shirt Dax moved to stand in front of her and give her some measure of privacy. He did it instinctively and without thinking, his back to the royal family, a deep snarl was the only thing he heard before the powerful arm of King Afua swept him up and slammed him against the far wall.

A battle yell left Dax's mouth as he executed a quick combat change. His sleek black panther attacked the massive lion of King Afua. Queen Layla held Sasha and Laini back while the men fought each other.

The king swiped out with his enormous paws, Dax could feel a breeze as he barely managed to avoid the blow. One hit from them and he knew there would be no coming back. The king was the largest Andovian Dax had ever seen, and any doubts he'd ever had that this man had ripped the arms off a man quickly fled. Weaving in between the kings legs Dax was able to trip him up, and with all the speed and dexterity he'd gained from hours of training onboard ship, he leapt on the kings back.

Gaining a foothold Dax started to close his jaw around the sensitive area behind the kings neck when with a move he'd never seen before the king threw Dax across the room. Dazed and seeing stars he struggled to stand up as the king advanced. A blur of motion caught his eye as Sasha sprung between her father and Dax.

Growling Dax tried to nudge her aside but nearly fell over when he did. He started to see spots and his panther receded in his mind. Naked his hand wrapped around Sasha's arm and he pulled her behind him. Facing the king, he barred his teeth and did his best to appear threatening while the ferocious menace bared down on them.

"Stop it now!" Sasha's voice was shrill and broke at the end. Consumed with fear for Dax's life she'd broke free from her mother and ran to stand between Dax and her father. As soon as she had she realized just how huge her father was. His face a mask of rage, the king threw back his head and let out an ear drum shattering roar. Dax somehow managed to hold his ground while Sasha tried desperately not to pee her pants.

The only other cat she'd seen was Dax and he was barely half the size of her father. Did she get that big? Taking a deep breath, she tried to calm down. She knew she'd never break free from Dax's vice like grip on her arm so she poked her head around his body and glared at her father. His face was so close it was almost pressing into Dax's bare chest and the growl coming from his mouth caused the floor to vibrate under their feet. Reaching out Sasha slapped her father's nose. "Bad kitty."

King Afua stopped growling and sat back on his haunches with a look of extreme surprise on his face. The room, already very tense, somehow became even more so. Dax backed up until she was pressed into the wall on one side and his naked body on the other. Any other time, with the mating heat as high as it was, she wouldn't have been able to control her roaming hands, but the fear in the room was enough to quell her lust.

The change came over her father and he stood in the middle of the room naked. Blushing Sasha looked away and wished desperately that when you changed back to your human form you had clothes on. Stepping forward Queen Layla offered her husband a robe that must have been laying around for just such an occasion. Standing beside him as he slipped it on she stared at Sasha who was still smushed into the wall. The queen's face was impassive and Sasha had no idea what she was thinking, not for the first time she realized she had no idea who these people really were.

Resting her head on Dax she closed her eyes and wished they were back on Earth. Anywhere but this strange place where she had family that morphed into house sized lions and attacked the man she loved for trying to save her from the embarrassment of standing in front of them nude. If she wasn't so tired and hungry she would be giving them a piece of her mind, who cared if they were royalty.

Why wasn't she telling them off? Her father acted like a giant bully, literally. What did it matter that she hadn't slept in over two days and all she'd had during that time was a bowl of the best soup ever created.

Channeling her lioness, she pushed against Dax with a surprising amount of strength managing to move him enough to slip out. Wearing just Dax's t-shirt she stood in front of her parents hands on her hips.

"I've been on Andove for over forty-eight hours, that's Earth time I have no idea what it is here, anyway, during that time I have not been given the opportunity to sleep and I've only been fed one bowl of soup. It was life changing soup, but still. Then when I finally meet my family my father attacks my mate."

The word felt foreign on her tongue. Everything she had just said actually did, but she wasn't finished.

"Clearly Andove is not known for its great hospitality, or maybe it's just the felines, but if we aren't given some kind of accommodation or at least the ability to leave and find our own in the next two minutes. I'm going to... I don't know what I'm going to do, but it won't be pretty."

Deflated she leaned back into the solid wall that was Dax, who had stepped up behind her somewhere in the middle of her barely coherent tirade. Near tears she added, "If I wasn't so damn tired I would have you cowering where you stand. I've been known to be a real terror back on Earth and everyone knows not to mess with me."

Sweeping her up into his arms Dax faced the royal family and waited for any kind of response. They were standing as a united front across from him, their emotions hidden behind a royal mask. When they said nothing he backed out of the room, making sure not to offend anyone this time and took Sasha away.

Chapter Sixteen

Walking through the palace, naked, when he came to a
robe station he grabbed one before making his way to
the porter they had used to get there. Dialing in
coordinates he had memorized, within seconds they
were standing outside the small flat he kept in Galia for
the rare moments he was on planet.

Fighting to remain conscience, but barely
hanging on, Sasha asked, "Where are we? Are we going
back to the ship?"

Walking up the three flights of stairs while
holding her and still recovering from his fight with the
king it took Dax a minute to answer. "We're at my
place. It's not much, and it's been a couple of years, but
it should be clean. I hope."

Putting his thumbprint to a panel the door to
his apartment slid open revealing, thankfully, that it was
clean, though, a bit musty. Walking across the threshold
holding Sasha he felt a surge of possessiveness. He'd
been on the ship for a long time, but it never quite felt
like more than just a ship. This, however, was home
and it felt right bringing Sasha here.

Crossing the living space with its minimal
decorations he took her to the bedroom and gently laid
her down on his bed. She had already fallen asleep and

as soon as she hit mattress she spread out until she covered most of the massive bed. Chuckling he tossed the robe and joined her.

Exhausted he missed the blinking light letting him know that someone had tried to contact him. Since his tablet had been confiscated as soon as they'd been taken to the testing facility he'd been off the grid for well over two days, but he'd been so wrapped up in Sasha he'd forgotten the other members of their group and their mission. Slipping off to sleep he snuggled close to Sasha and buried his nose in her neck surrounding himself with her scent.

Hours later Sasha woke up to an insistent beeping. Groaning she rolled over and tried to smack her alarm clock, but it wasn't there. Prying her eyelids apart, she took in the strange room around her and everything that had happened slowly started to force its way back into her mind. Groaning she covered her eyes with her hands and tried to forget it all.

When she felt fingers pushing up the shirt she was wearing her eyes flew open and she met Dax's gaze. The mating heat flared up and she pushed his hands aside. Straddling him she looked down at his sleepy gaze and marveled at how much she had grown to love him in such a short time. She knew part of it was her lioness, but when he'd stepped between her and her uber scary father something in her had clicked. No one had ever done that for her before. She was always the one protecting, she was never the protected.

Her fingers found the bottom of the shirt and she slowly dragged it over her body, revealing her bare breasts as she did. Dax groaned underneath her and he reached up to cup her with his hands. His thumbs brushed across the tights buds of her nipples and she sucked in a quick breath. The fire that had been banked since they landed on Andove roared to life and she dropped her head down so that she could capture his lips with her own.

Their tongues danced together as they tried to taste every inch of each other. Dax's hands moved to the junction between her thighs and found that her pussy was already wet and ready for him. Moving his hands to her waist he lifted her up and moved her down his chest until his jutting cock pressed against her. Her mouth paused over his lips and her hand traveled south to grab his stiff pole. She slowly began brushing the tip of his sword across her soaked pussy lips. When it brushed her tender clit she jumped. Swirling his cock against her eager slit, within seconds she was panting. Her body burning up with a desperate need to feel him inside.

"Oh god, Dax, I need you. Fuck me. Fuck me now."

As he plunged her down onto his cock the force of her orgasm rocked her body. Stars danced in her vision and her body vibrated from the energy of her release. Thrusting hard into her, Dax's own orgasm burst from him much faster than he wanted, but it was phenomenal and he immediately started planning what he was going to do to her in his custom built shower stall.

Collapsed on his chest, Sasha could still feel his cock inside of her, and even with the tremors of her orgasm quaking through her body, she was ready for the next round. Nibbling on his neck, he began slowly thrusting into her, she moaned as she made her way up to his ear.

Preparing to whisper something incredibly

naughty the incessant beeping that had woken her up pushed through the haze of lust. Sitting up she asked, "What is that horrible beeping noise?"

Keeping his pace, Dax's strokes remained steady, reaching out he cupped her breasts swaying in front of him. His thumb brushed across her nipple and a small gasp escaped her lips. The speed of his thrusts quickened as his lips surrounded her erect bud. Her head fell back before she could lose her train of thought again she asked, "Dax, what is that beeping?"

Rolling over on top of her, Dax's lips left her breasts and he answered, "It's the doorbell."

She froze underneath him, "What?"

He covered her lips with his own, claiming her mouth, his body rocked into hers while his hand moved between them to find her clit. Strumming at her sensitive button Sasha's mind scattered and all she could focus on was the way he was masterfully playing her body. He knew exactly what to do to push her to the peak and just when she couldn't take anymore his well-timed thrust had her screaming out his name.

Hot and sweaty with the smell of sex in the air Sasha felt every inch the cat she was, wanting to stretch out and bask in the afterglow of their lovemaking. Their scents were completely combined and she felt a click in her mind as their mating bond snapped into place. A flood of foreign emotions filled her mind. All the pleasure and contentment she had been feeling was doubled. The strongest emotion, though, was love. It was awe-inspiring because of its sheer magnitude.

Her body reeling she was barely able to prop herself up to look to where Dax had rolled off of her. "Do you feel this? Is that all you?"

Tears had filled her eyes, partly from an intense

headache that was pounding at her brain, but also because she was seeing herself through his eyes and there was no way she deserved to be seen that way. He thought of her as a warrior goddess, gorgeous but ready and willing to come to anyone's defense.

His own head splitting from the sudden connection he answered, "Of course that's how I see you. I had no idea you saw me as a roguish pirate protecting you from harm. Who is this Han Solo you keep associating with me in your mind? Do I need to find and kill him?"

Turning beet red Sasha buried her head in a pillow. Pulling the pillow down she said, "Don't ever say anything to anyone about that or I will..."

He propped himself up on his elbow to look down at her. Tracing the swell of her breast, he smiled as she tried to think of a suitable threat. "I promise love I won't mention anything to anyone ever." He could feel her relief through their bond and his smile grew. This was like nothing he'd ever expected, a mating bond this strong was rare, rarer than finding your true mate even. It just proved that his cat had made the right choice in mating with Sasha.

She could feel how smug he felt through their bond but didn't need it to tell her what he felt, his smugness was all over his face, and she knew exactly when he picked up on her exasperation with him. His smile was so cocky and even as she was rolling her eyes she was thinking that it was cute. When he laughed she knew he had picked up on that.

Groaning she rolled out of bed and was preparing to take a shower, alone, when she noticed the beeping again. "Wait, did you say that's the doorbell?"

Lying on the bed naked, his cock already slightly

erect just from seeing her naked, he grinned, "Yup. I don't know why they keep on ringing they should be able to scent that we were busy."

"Oh my god are you serious?! Why didn't you tell me? If I had known we wouldn't have just had sex, twice while people were on your doorstep."

"Babe you need to get used to it. We can make soundproof rooms, but scent proof hasn't been done yet. At least not well enough for a trained Andovian."

Growling she looked around for something to put on before opening the door but she didn't have any clothes here. Grabbing the robe Dax had taken from the palace she quickly put it on before moving to the front of the apartment. Dax took his time pulling on sweatpants because he knew she wouldn't know how to use the door. When he walked out into his living room she was standing in front of it frowning.

"You know this is a fire hazard. What if you were unconscious and I needed to get us out of the building?"

"It would never happen."

Stomping her foot in irritation she replied, "You don't know that, what if it did? How would I open the door? There's no door knob, it doesn't appear to be motion censored like on the ship, there isn't even some kind of futuristic plate I put my thumb too."

He gave her a cocky smile as he said, "Open."

The door slid open revealing a royal guard. His face lost the cocky smile as he pulled Sasha back behind him. Baring his teeth he asked, "What do you want?"

"We're here to bring the princess back to the palace. Step aside dog."

His hackles raised the only thing keeping Dax from attacking at the insult was Sasha standing behind him, except that she wasn't standing behind him. A blur shot in front of him and he realized too late to stop her that Sasha was attacking the guard. As a threat approached him the guard's training took over, but Sasha hadn't been raised in the best environment and she was able to easily evade his defenses. Her hand, now with lengthened claws, scraped across the man's body.

The smell of blood filled the air and the mist began to surround the guard. Grabbing Sasha around the waist and throwing her into the apartment, Dax ran for his weapons stash, but he was too late. The large cougar that the guard changed into pounced on him. At the disadvantage, Dax tried to avoid the claws and teeth until he could make his move. A huge roar filled the air and the massive paw of Sasha's lioness batted the cougar and shot him across the room. Hitting the wall hard he was out cold and the mist surrounded him leaving behind the naked guard.

Sasha in her lioness form paced the room, growling and snarling while Dax slowly stood. He could feel through their mating bond just how furious she was and how scared she'd been when the cougar had attacked him.

"Sasha, love, I'm alright. Just a couple scratches I'll be fine." He slowly approached her, making soft soothing sounds to try and calm her down. Just as he reached her side and she lowered her head to his chest the sound of boots marching up the stairwell came to their ears.

Jerking away from him she was at the door in an instant. As the first guard stepped foot on the landing she let out a heart stopping roar. The guard unable to stand the sound fell to his knees in front of her. She raised her paw, claws out, and was prepared to swipe him across the face, possibly killing him in the process.

Dax moved to block her, "Sasha no. You can't hurt them, they're just obeying orders. Orders that your parents probably gave them."

She snarled, clearly unhappy, but she lowered her paw as the rest of the guard filed up the stairs. The man Sasha had been about to attack was pulled back as a new guard took his place. Addressing Sasha the man said, "We're here by order of King Afua to take you back to the palace."

Unsure what she would do, especially with the curt tone the man was taking with her, Dax had to fight back a laugh when she yawned. Every single one of her sharp teeth on display. He could see the guard who'd spoken swallow in concern.

"Enough."

A loud, firm voice came from the floor below. The line of guards parted as Prince Amiri moved forward. Frowning at Sasha, who towered over him in her lioness form, he ordered her to change. Dax bowed before the prince and silently pleaded Sasha to do what he told her.

If King Afua had a violent reputation it was nothing compared to Prince Amiri and Dax had seen the princes' actions first hand. Feeling his plea through their bond Sasha bared her teeth at her brother and then turned around, flicking her tail at him as she moved back into the apartment. Dax could scent her change and then heard her find the robe she'd been wearing and slip it on. Her face was a mask that perfectly hid her emotions, just like the ones her parents had worn yesterday, and if it wasn't for their bond he would have had no idea how nervous she was, or how pissed.

"So I have a brother now. Are there any more family members I need to know about? A crazy uncle, perhaps? How about some grandparents to spoil me, that would be nice."

"You could stand to learn some manners. Were you raised by barbarians? You should kneel before your prince."

"I kneel before no one, least of all a pompous jackass I've never met before."

Growling the prince took a step toward Sasha with murder in his eyes. Dax was still on his knees at Sasha's side and he tensed ready to leap in front of her if the prince took another step. His slight movement brought the princes attention to him and a look of disgust crossed his face.

"Do you know who you've aligned yourself with? Has the dog told you what he's done? Or did he mate you before telling you?"

Eyes flashing gold Sasha responded, "Don't you dare insult my mate. I know about his past, that he was dishonorably discharged for something he didn't do."

Snorting her brother responded, "So he gave you a sob story. The pathetic excuse for a cat kneeling beside you was accused of rape. The only reason he wasn't imprisoned is because the evidence was circumstantial, but the minute he was free he ran, and if that doesn't prove his guilt I don't know what does."

Sasha tensed beside him at the accusation. In her eyes, rape was one of the worst things you could ever do to someone. Growing up she had known a couple kids that had the misfortune of being placed in worse foster homes than she. The look in their eyes haunted her and was one of the major reasons she had become a lawyer. She knew that Dax would never force himself on anyone and take that power away from them. When she had been at her most vulnerable he had held her while she cried instead of making her carry out the seduction she had started.

Resting her hand on his shoulder Sasha could feel the worry coming from their bond, she squeezed lightly to reassure him. "Lies. Anyone that knows Dax would know those are lies. He would never force anyone." She snorted, "Not to stroke his ego, but he would never have too. Have you looked at him?"

There were a couple snickers from the guards and the prince snarled quickly quieting them down. "I'm not going to argue with a woman going through a mating heat, you're obviously unable to listen to reason. Now get your things we're going to the palace."

"You're one to talk about manners. If you think I'm going to leave with you after the way you've acted you're crazy."

"Akali you will come with me now!"

The force of his shout was enough to rock Sasha back on her heels and his words sparked another ember of anger. Shaking her head she replied, "I'm getting tired of people calling me that, my name is Sasha."

"Your name is Akali and I refuse to use the name your kidnappers gave you."

She pursed her lips at that comment, she hadn't thought of it that way. Feeling deflated she sagged against Dax, she was so tired of all of this. She just wanted to find her place in this new life, but so far most of her glimpses of royalty were not positive. Why couldn't she just live with Dax?

Leaning into her legs while still remaining on his knees Dax tried to send soothing feelings through their bond. It had been years since he'd seen the prince and he didn't remember him being this over the top. The Prince Amiri he'd met was calm until pushed, this man was anything but.

"Dax is coming with me."

Clenching his teeth, the prince shot Dax a look of absolute hate, before dipping his head in agreement. Turning his back he marched down the stairs while ordering the guards to wait for them to get ready. Moving back into the apartment Sasha slammed the door behind.

"Oh my god that man is not related to me. I refuse to be associated to a bully." She crossed her arms and frowned at the door. Pulling her into his arms Dax rubbed his hands up and down her arms as he tried to calm her down, but it wasn't working. Moving away from him she stomped into his bedroom and began rummaging through his clothes.

Deciding that the joint shower he'd been hoping for was not going to happen Dax settled for a quick sonic cleanse. Stepping out of the stall he found Sasha waiting to take his place. She muttered under her breath the entire time and when she stepped out she was even angrier.

Grabbing her around the waist Dax pressed his naked body into hers.

"I am so not in the mood right now."

Chuckling he rubbed his hands up and down her body. Bending his head down he nibbled at her neck while she stood there tapping her foot. Stepping back he was grinning when he answered her, "I just want to make sure my scent is all over you so no one gets any ideas."

She glanced pointedly down at his erect penis.

"I can't help what you do to me babe."

Rolling her eyes, she couldn't stop the smile that quirked her lips up. "Do you have any clothes that aren't cargo pants or sweats? I'd really prefer not to go back to the palace in a robe."

Swaggering across the room, not at all embarrassed by his hard cock, Dax opened a drawer nestled into the wall and tossed her a dress. Holding it up she raised her eyebrow at him, "I'm not even going to ask why you have this."

He gave her a cocky grin before getting dressed himself. Minutes later they were stepping out, arm and arm, and being led down to the waiting prince. Sasha was surprised to see a vehicle waiting for them. "Why aren't we porting? Wouldn't that be faster?"

The prince adjusted his sleeve not meeting her eyes, "I prefer to use a more physical means of transportation than to have my atoms scattered all over the place."

Somehow she knew he was lying but no one else appeared to pick up on that. Glancing at Dax he just shrugged his shoulders and held the door open for her. Sliding into the cool air-conditioned back seat Sasha took in all the luxury. It wasn't all that different from the one time she'd ridden in a limo. Though, things were just slightly off. There was a fridge unit, but it was more bubble shaped than a cube and all the little buttons were labeled with symbols she didn't recognize. Sighing she wondered if she would ever get use to all the new technology and just how different everything was.

Moving in beside her Dax took her hand in his

and gave it a reassuring squeeze. "You mastered the shower stall with no problems, just give yourself time and you'll pick up on everything."

They both paused and then looked at each other in surprise. She hadn't spoken her concerns out loud he'd picked up on her thoughts through their mating bond. Was he able to read her mind?

Shaking his head no he answered, "I couldn't read your mind and it wasn't a thought, it was more like a very specific feeling."

"Then how did you know what I was thinking just now?"

He laughed and pulled her close, "It was very obvious from your face what you were thinking. I love you Sasha, but I don't want you to be able to read my thoughts any more than you want me to be able to read yours."

They were cuddling in the back of the vehicle when Prince Amiri joined them. He frowned from across the back of the car at them. When the door was closed behind him and they moved into traffic, his face changed completely. Leaning forward he took both of their hands in his and rested his forehead against them.

"Forgive me, my friend and sister. I'm sorry I had to act that way, but there is much I have to tell in a very short time."

Looking at Dax in surprise he gave her an impish smile. Pulling her hand out of the princes she said, "What the hell is happening here?"

"I think Prince Amiri should explain because I'm as in the dark as you."

Crossing her arms she replied, "It doesn't look that way."

"Don't be mad at Dax, Akali, that's just the way

he is."

"Wait you know him? Seriously someone better start explaining what is going on or I'm going to get really pissed off and I don't have enough control to stop my lioness from taking over."

"If you'll be quiet I'll tell you."

Frowning at her brother she settled back into the seat and waited for him to tell her exactly what was going on.

Leaning forward Amiri began his story, "First I want to apologize to you Dax, I was off planet or I would have done everything I could to stop your discharge. Though, now that I know more of what is going on, it's better that I wasn't available."

Glancing over at Dax she could see that he thought differently but then he reached out and took her hand. Placing a kiss on her knuckles she could feel through their bond that he was fine with what had happened because it brought him to her. Blushing she returned her attention to her brother in time to see him rolling his eyes. It was uncanny how similar the response was to her own.

"Back to the matter at hand. As soon as I returned to Andove and was told what happened to you I began to look into things. I quickly discovered that there was more going on. The more I learned the more I realized that there is an entire faction in the government and military focused on overthrowing my father and myself. There have been multiple attempts on my life and the life of the king. I've stopped using porters because of one of those attempts. It seems that nothing is safe.

"There are only a handful of people I trust and I have been unable to see how far up the faction has infiltrated. I'm afraid that someone in our inner circle has betrayed us. Certain communications have been intercepted and several people close to me have been killed and the only people that knew of them were family.

"I'm sorry Akali you've shown up at a very dangerous time, but I'd like to use that to our advantage. If we can discover who exactly in the inner circle has betrayed us we'd be much closer to ending this faction once and for all."

"You want to use me as bait in some way, don't you?"

He smiled at her and leaned back into the seat. He quickly laid out his plan as the car zipped through the streets and came closer to the palace. After Amiri explained his plan Sasha sat quietly and she mulled it over. There wasn't too much risk to her, or so it seemed, but she knew that Dax was not happy about it and feared for her safety.

Ignoring Amiri she turned to Dax, "I've never backed down from anything in my life so I want to help, but I don't know this world and there isn't time to make an informed decision, so I need your help. Are my father and brother good men? Is our country, kingdom, whatever it's called, better in their hands?"

Sensing that he shouldn't say anything, Amiri stayed quiet. If anyone else had implied that he wouldn't be a good ruler he would have been greatly offended, but it gave him a feeling of pride that his sister would ask such an important question. That she didn't trust him immediately just because he was her brother made him happy. Their world was not a world that allowed them that luxury.

"I've fought beside your brother. He is a

violent, sometimes vicious man, but he is also loyal and protects his people. I don't know if I would call him a good man, but he is dedicated and strong and he and the king are the best options for our people."

Staring into Dax's eyes, feeling all his emotions through their bond, she nodded her head. Turning back to Amiri she said, "I'll do it."

Chapter Seventeen

When they arrived at the palace, as soon as they exited the vehicle, Amiri picked up his regal, arrogant act. He didn't wait for them as he strode up the palace steps and through the entryway. Trailing behind Sasha and Dax did their best to appear pissed off and unhappy about being there.

Amiri led them back to the same parlor they had been in the day before. King Afua and Queen Layla were waiting for them, as well as Laini and Ariel. Bowing to his father Amiri announced, "I have brought my sister, Akali, back home. She refused to leave the dog though."

"Amiri, please, we want your sister to feel welcomed." Standing up her mother moved forward and pulled Sasha into her arms. Unsure what to do Sasha kept her arms to her side. She could feel her mother's disappointment, but she was still not sure how to react around these people. What if her mother was the traitor? Stepping back the queen moved to stand beside her husband, who was flanked by Amiri and Laini. Ariel stood to the side, clearly she knew something was off but apparently hadn't heard of the fight between Dax and the king.

"You've got me here, what do you want now?"

Sasha's chin jutted out and she dared anyone to make a comment about her tone. As soon as they'd entered the room Dax had kneeled and as hard as she tugged he refused to stand up. "Does my mate have to kneel before you the entire time or is he free to stand?"

Ariel growled at her, "Your mate is an accused rapist and does not deserve to be in the presence of royalty."

Rolling her eyes, Sasha answered in a bored voice, "Yes, so that's what they tell me, but I've yet to see proof. I may have only known him a short time, but Dax would never hurt a woman."

Snorting in disgust Ariel walked to the wall and with a few clicks a hidden screen came to life. She pulled Dax's record up, including images of a woman that had been beaten. Then she hit play on a video recording of the woman going into detail about what Dax had done to her. It was gruesome, and Sasha couldn't help the tears that filled her eyes. She knew it was a doctored video, Amiri had already told her about its existence, but that didn't make the woman's story any less heartbreaking. She slowly moved away from Dax as the poor woman's testimony played.

"Enough." Walking across the room Queen Layla stopped the video, glaring at Ariel she said, "There was no reason for that."

Bowing her head slightly, Ariel replied, "The princess needed to know what kind of man she has mated to. With the mating heat over they may now go their separate ways. She won't be able to mate again, but at least she won't have to be around the dog."

Sasha felt lost and alone. She stood between Dax and her family with no ties to either and with no idea what her future was going to hold. Still on his knees Dax started moving toward her. "Sasha please, let me explain."

When his hand touched her sleeve she jerked away, "Don't. I can't believe I... Just leave, I never want to speak to you again."

Still by the control panel Ariel pressed the intercom, "Send in guards we need some trash taken out."

Immediately guards entered the room. Grabbing Dax they dragged him from the room. He was screaming her name as he left and she flinched from the force of emotion she was feeling and receiving from their connection. As the doors slid closed the room filled with an unnatural silence. Wiping tears from her eyes, she stuck her chin out and faced her family.

"What now? I'm alone on a strange new world, with people who are evidently my family, but honestly you guys all act like a bunch of assholes, well, except for Laini."

Giving her a small smile Laini started to step forward but her father stopped her. "I know things have not been ideal for you Akali, but you are a princess of Andove and a feline. You will accept your new place with dignity and stop these outbursts."

Biting her tongue and keeping the retort that came to her lips back she dipped her head in acknowledgment.

"We have rooms set up for you. Clothes will be made for you and a tutor hired to take care of all the gaps in your education. Hopefully, there won't be too many things for you to unlearn."

Her hands made fists at the idea of having to go back to school. She fought back the urge to glance at Amiri standing behind her father. He had told her that this would be difficult, but they didn't know who was the mole. It could be Laini, Layla, or Ariel. Sasha's money was on Ariel, but Amiri wasn't so sure. Evidence had been found that could implicate any of the women. Laini and Layla had been the only nice ones to her so far, but from the stories Amiri told her they could be ruthless and she couldn't forget the emotionless masks they'd worn after Afua had attacked Dax.

"Laini take Akali to her quarters and make sure she's comfortable."

Sasha wanted to fight, it was her instinct, but she resisted. So far, everything was playing out exactly how Amiri said it would. As Laini led her through the palace she tried to pay attention, but the emotions coming from Dax were distracting her. He was angry and afraid for her, but it didn't feel like he was being hurt. The plan was for Amiri's men to take him, but with all the distrust going around who knew if that had actually worked. What if the guards that arrived when Ariel called were part of the faction?

Lost in her negative thoughts she tripped and the only thing that kept her from falling was Laini's hand steadying her. "Thanks."

Looking around the hall Laini's voice was barely more than a whisper when she spoke, "Akali I know this is hard right now, but things will get better. I promise."

Sasha gave her a small smile and tried to hide the sinking feeling in her stomach. Did this mean that Laini was part of the faction? She followed closely and tried to bring her focus back to the mission. She needed to find out who the mole was and then get that information to Amiri.

"Here we are." As Laini opened the ornate

double doors Sasha was struck with the simple beauty of the rooms provided to her. Stepping inside she gasped when she saw the amazing view. Unlike the view in the parlor, this was a view of a savannah spanning out far into the distance. Awestruck she forgot all about the secret war going on, the fact that Dax had been taken from her, everything. The waves of grass spoke to a side of herself she was only now becoming aware of. Inside her mind her lioness purred. The savannah was home.

"It's beautiful. We have places like this on Earth, but I never actually saw them."

Laini joined her by the window and they both stood in silence for a minute and just took the view in. Long before she was ready to Sasha backed away and brought her focus to the room around her. There wasn't much, but every item appeared to be high quality. Walking across the room she opened a door that led to her bedroom. The bed was huge and would easily accommodate her lioness if she ever got stuck in that form again.

When images of her and Dax rolling around naked on the sheets popped into her mind she closed the door and turned back to the sitting room. She shoved the deliciously naughty thoughts out of her mind as she started to feel Dax's arousal through their bond. She frowned, he better be aroused because of their connection. Stopping herself from going down that rabbit hole she looked to Laini who was studying her across the room.

"I'm sure you're tired. I can leave you."

Sasha wanted that, she desperately wanted to be alone with her thoughts, but that wasn't the plan. Forcing a smile, she said, "Actually I'm pretty hungry.

Really hungry. Could you take me to the kitchens."

"Or we could just order food up. I could have the royal wardrobe mistress show you your new clothes while we eat."

She seemed so hopeful and eager at the prospect that Sasha couldn't' say no, even though the idea of trying on a bunch of clothes sounded like hell to her.

"That sounds perfect."

Smiling Laini let out a little squeal as she went to the panel on the wall and began calling people. When the food arrived shortly thereafter Sasha was surprised at how loud her stomach growled when she scented the food. Blushing she said, "I guess I was even hungrier than I thought."

Sitting down at the table that had been quickly arranged, Sasha dug in. The food was unfamiliar, but she was so hungry it didn't matter. Moaning when she bit into a piece of something particularly good she didn't remember Laini was there until she started laughing.

"I'm sorry it's rude, but you seem to really be enjoying everything."

Blushing Sasha swallowed what was in her mouth and tried to slow down.

"I shouldn't have said anything, please, eat. I'm sure your famished, everyone normally is after a mating. There isn't much time to spend on eating."

Dropping her eyes, Sasha knew there was no way she could blush any redder. Everyone seemed to be so much more comfortable with their sexuality here. She would never have joked about sex with a sister, maybe Anika, probably Anika, but no one else. Anika. Damn, she'd completely forgotten about her friend. She hoped they were okay and had found Kelly. If they didn't get things taken care of here on Andove quickly she would have to find a way to contact them.

"I've done it again. I shouldn't have said anything about your mate. Please forgive me?"

Sasha had forgotten that Laini was there, again. Mentally kicking herself at how horrible she was as a spy she tried to think of something to say but was saved when a low bell rang announcing someone at the door. She smiled at Laini before saying,"Come in."

A stream of people began filing through the door, eyes wide she wished briefly that she'd finished her food before it was taken away from her and a thin, dramatic woman began displaying one beautiful garment after another to her.

"I don't know which I should choose they're all so wonderful."

Looking distressed the wardrobe mistress spoke, "I'm so terribly sorry your highness, you misunderstand. You don't have to pick one, they are all for you. I was merely asking which one you wanted to try on first."

"Oh." Feeling lost she looked to Laini who was giving her a huge grin, clearly she was enjoying herself. Sasha swallowed down a knot of tears at the fact that she was being given so much and stood up to make her first selection.

Hours later Sasha was amazed that she had actually ended up having fun. In their girliest of moments, Anika and she had talked about one day making enough money to go out on a shopping spree. This was almost as good as what they imagined, she just wished Anika had been here. She wasn't sure if she was going to be able to wait until this whole uncover the mole thing played out. She needed to know what was going on with her friend.

Escorting Laini out of her room she was distracted and almost missed what she was saying.

"I know this is going to be rough, dad can be a tyrant sometimes, so can Amiri, but things will get better. I'll take care of them. You don't have to worry."

Giving her a quick kiss on the cheek Laini left Sasha alone and wondering just how her sister was going to take care of the king and crown prince.

Chapter Eighteen

Sunning herself on a rock in the middle of the savannah she felt like she was home. This was everything she had ever wanted. She was exactly where she belonged and she knew that eventually Sasha would grow to love it, Dax would make sure of that.

Purring at the thought of their mate she reached out through their bond to check on him and that's when she realized something was wrong. He was in pain. Leaping up she started running through the tall grass, leaping over anything in her way. She had to get to her mate.

Racing at top speed, his scent the only thing guiding her, she cursed her other half for agreeing to this plan. They had known it was dangerous but never had she thought he would be the one in danger. His scent grew fainter and fainter until it disappeared, the only thing letting her know he was still alive was their bond.

Sasha woke up with a roar in her throat. Throwing back the covers she stumbled across the room to the communications panel. She desperately tried to contact Dax, she'd been told not to, but after that dream she had to make sure he was okay. Nothing. She tried to get Amiri, but he didn't answer either. She had no one else to contact that she could trust. She briefly thought about talking to the king, but had no idea if he had been included in their plans.

Throwing on clothes she decided that she was just going to find him on her own. Slipping out into the dark hallway she paused a moment and listened for anyone. She knew there were guards around, but she hadn't seen any in the private quarters. It was possible, though, that they used cameras. Taking a chance she bolted down the corridor toward the porter.

She decided to go for speed rather than stealth and ran flat out through the hallways. Just as she reached the corridor the porter was off of she heard the echo of boots marching toward her. Peeking around the corner whoever was coming was not yet in view. It was now or never. She raced down the hallway and ended up going too fast, sliding into her turn she slammed into the wall. The air was knocked from her lungs and she stumbled forward trying not to lose her momentum.

Falling into the porting chamber she was just entering the coordinates when a stream of guards entered her view. Someone called out her name as she disappeared.

Stepping out of the porting tube she had no idea how long she had before they followed her. Looking up at Dax's apartment she couldn't tell if anyone was there from the street. He was supposed to be here. That was the plan. When the guards escorted him out of the palace he was supposed to return here and wait for her. Keying in the code he'd given her she took the steps two at a time as she made her way up to his landing. When she got there the door was locked, once more entering his code, she burst through to find he wasn't there.

Fighting down a scream of frustration she took

a deep breath and realized that he hadn't been there
since they'd left together. Walking through the place to
confirm what her nose was telling her she found
everything exactly how it had been when they'd left.
The guards hadn't let him go home, which meant either
they hadn't been Amiri's guards or Amiri was not on
their side.

Growling in frustration she tried to figure out
her next move. She had no way of finding Dax and no
one she could trust. This was not how things were
supposed to play out. Looking down at the street a
large transport filled with guards landed just as they also
started pouring out of the porter.

"Shit."

Preparing to run she missed the man creeping
up behind her. She was just turning around when out of
the corner of her eye she saw a bolt of light coming
straight for her. Crumpling to the ground her lioness
roared inside her head but as Sasha slipped into
unconsciousness there was nothing either of them
could do.

Chapter Nineteen

A noxious odor right underneath her nose finally woke Sasha. Slowly sitting up she discovered that she was in the back of a vehicle very similar to the one that Amiri had used. Blinking she glanced around the dark interior and tried to remember how she got there. The last thing she remembered was being in Dax's apartment and then… someone shot her!

"Good you're awake."

Her eyes darted to the darkest corner of the car where for the first time she noticed someone sitting. A light clicked on and her aunt was illuminated.

"Ariel? What's going on?"

Sasha's mind raced, there was so much going on, and she wasn't sure who to trust, but all that mattered was Dax. If Ariel was a part of the faction then the last thing she needed to know was how much Dax meant to Sasha. Trying to calm her breathing she rubbed the back of her head where a pounding headache was building.

"I'm sorry my dear, I never meant for you to be hurt. The man I sent was overzealous in executing my orders. There is much I must tell you, but first I need to know, why were you out of the palace so late? As much as I would love it to be, Galia is not a safe place at night for someone like you."

The best lies always held a grain of truth, if she wanted Ariel to believe her, she needed to make this as believable as possible. She had no problem looking concerned and pained when she said, "I was sleeping, but I woke up because I was in pain. I didn't understand at first because there didn't seem to be anything wrong, but it just got worse. It was like someone was beating me only I was alone."

She paused and bit her lip before continuing, doing her best to appear innocent and stupid, "I thought it might have something to do with my mating bond with Dax. I thought he was hurting me on purpose. I went to his house to get him to stop."

Frowning at her Ariel asked, "You've formed a bond with him? I knew you two were mated, but I didn't realize it was a true mating. That complicates things."

Shaking her head to appear confused, it was a physical effort not to roll her eyes and keep up the dumb act, "A true mating? Aren't bonds normal on Andove? I don't understand Aunt Ariel."

When Ariel's eyes narrowed she thought she might have pushed it too far and rubbed her head and tried to fix a dazed look in her eyes. Hopefully, Ariel would chalk any suspicions she had to Sasha being stunned.

"True matings are extremely rare my dear, but we can work around it. First I need to know, do you love him? I know that your cat is telling you that you do, but you must push past that, what do you feel for him?"

What did she feel for Dax? She loved him and it wasn't just her cat saying that. The man was gorgeous yes, but he was funny in an annoying way, and he was smart, and he was loyal to his friends. He took care of her but didn't smother her. He was exactly what she had always wanted in a man and he'd just showed up out of the blue from another planet. It was incredible, but she fought down those feelings in case love somehow had a scent and Ariel picked up on it.

She squinted her eyes and put all the anger she was feeling at being out of control into her words, "I hate him. He forced me into a mating I didn't understand and now I'm forever connected to a man that brutalizes women. I worked with battered women a lot when I was on Earth and the fact that I am now connected to him makes me physically ill."

Her words were forceful and filled with rage, she held Ariel's gaze through her entire rant, but dropped her eyes when she whispered, "I wish he were dead."

As soon as the words were out she wished she'd never said them. An intense feeling of impending doom settled around her. She'd never believed in jinxes before, but as soon as the words left her lips she'd felt like a curse was now floating in the air. Concerned she glanced back up at Ariel, hoping that her words had at least been what Ariel wanted to hear.

They were, smiling at Sasha, Ariel said, "That's good to know. Since you are the true mate of that vile cat things are going to be more difficult, but not impossible. Though, I am afraid that you will experience some pain, but once we're finished you'll be free of him forever. You'd like that, won't you?"

"Yes of course." Sasha tried to appear eager but a knot formed in her throat and she was having difficulty swallowing. Looking out the window at the passing city she wished desperately for someone to help her. Amiri was supposed to have men watching her, but she'd never seen them. She hoped that they had been able to follow her to Dax's house and see her being kidnaped.

After several minutes of silence where Sasha thought of every horrible scenario that could play out, she couldn't take it anymore and asked, "Are we going back to the palace?"

"No, my dear. I'm taking you to Dax."

"Why? I thought I wouldn't have to deal with him anymore." She tried to appear annoyed at the prospect while inside she was jumping for joy. Something was finally going right.

"There is more going on here than simply your relationship with a rapist. The kingdom is going through a very turbulent time. It's really too much to go into right now, but your appearance has complicated matters."

"I'm sorry?"

"It's alright my dear, I always plan on the unexpected happening. I've already figured out a way to use you to my advantage."

"That's good, how will I be able to help?"

"We'll go into that later my dear. Right now, you need your rest. Just sit back and try and sleep. We'll arrive in less than an hour."

Ariel switched the light off and the car was once again plunged into darkness, the only light was coming through the darkly tinted windows. Settling back Sasha tried not to think about the danger she was in or the pain that had intensified from Dax's side of the bond. It was clear that Ariel was the mole Amiri was searching for but did he know that?

Alone all Sasha could do was hope once she got

to Dax they could find a way to escape. Surprisingly her eyes had started to droop when the car jerked to a halt. A minute later the door was opened and warm air invaded the air-conditioned coolness of the car. Stepping out Ariel started giving orders to the people waiting. Someone reached in and grabbed Sasha's arm roughly and pulled her out.

"Hey, watch it, I can get out of a car on my own."

Ignoring her comment a big burly man that was built like a tank continued to keep a tight grip on her forearm, almost dragging her as he followed Ariel into a massive warehouse. They continued down a tight hall, through the few open doors she passed Sasha saw some labs, but the most disturbing thing was what she smelled. For every open door they passed showing techs working with test tubes and screens filled with data, they passed multiple closed doors that reeked of fear and unwashed bodies. What was going on here?

Finally, Ariel stopped at a closed door, she turned to study Sasha, who tried to appear calm and stupid but failed miserably. Ariel's gaze was shrewd and picked up on Sasha's distress, "There's nothing to worry about dear. This is a testing facility, all above board I promise.

"Now what I have to show you may be distressing, but please keep in mind those horrible things that Dax did to that unfortunate woman."

She opened the door and waited for Sasha's handler to drag her into the room before following. Dax was alone in the middle of a stark gray room. He was in a heap in the middle of the floor, blood everywhere, she could see his bones broken and sticking out in several places. She gagged at the sight and tears poured from her eyes, the only thing keeping her from running to him was the beast holding her back.

"Why have you done this to him?"

"Doesn't he deserve it? Didn't you want to see him dead?"

Dax groaned at her words and Sasha sent soothing feelings to him through their bond. His skin was ashy white and she couldn't see his eyes from her angle, the only thing that let her know that he was still alive, other than their bond, was the slight rise of his chest with every labored breath.

"I was angry, no one deserves this treatment. No one."

"Do I need to replay the video again? Do you need to hear what he did to that poor defenseless woman?"

She fought back the urge to tell Ariel she knew it was fake. They were both alive so she still had hope that someone would save them. She didn't want to blow her cover and ruin possibly giving Amiri the element of surprise. Though, where was Amiri? Why had he let this happen to Dax? Nothing was going as he'd planned and it looked like she and Dax were getting the short end of the stick.

"If we use torture aren't we no better than he is?"

Snorting Ariel responded, "So naive, is that what you learned growing up on that backwater? That violence is wrong? You are a lioness, a hunter, violence is what you're good at."

Frowning Sasha shook her head. "No, that's not true. I'm not only a lioness, I am more than just that side of myself. This is wrong."

"I was afraid that you would react this way. You were tainted by your time off planet, thankfully I had a plan if that were to be the case. You will still be of some use to me. Sadly you're going to suffer a fatal accident, the nation will mourn, but once word leaks out that you were mated to a rapist they will be outraged and the king will be forced to step down. The royal family may have some suspicions but when I tell them about how you slipped your protective guard and went traipsing around a city you knew nothing about they will believe me. In the end, after all my hard work and planning, I will finally gain my rightful title of Queen."

Shocked at the over the top evil monolog Sasha was unable to maintain her balance when the brute holding her tossed her into the middle of the room beside Dax.

As soon as they left Sasha moved to him. His wounds were even worse up close. Crying she tried to feel his pulse but it was weak and their bond was growing faint. She reached for his hand, his knuckles were bloody, but at least he didn't appear to have any broken bones.

"I love you, Dax, please don't die. Please. I don't want to be here without you. I need you."

Sobbing now she lost control and her lioness took over. As soon as the mist of change disappear she let out a ground-shaking roar of rage. Lowering her head she rammed the door with all the speed she could build in the small room and it crumpled underneath her. In the hallway, she shook her head to clear the stars from her eyes before turning to the oncoming threat. Five men decked out in combat gear and armed with weapons were rushing down the hall.

She charged down the hallway toward them. As she came closer they dropped to their knees and raised their weapons but they had misjudged her intent. In one long graceful leap, she was over their weapons and they were just a millisecond too slow in their adjustment to hit her. Landing behind them her back legs kicked out knocking three of them across the hall. They hit hard and slumped to the ground unconscious.

Two men remained and they had their weapons trained on Sasha. Snarling at them her paw, claws out, slashed out. She wasn't fast enough and one of the men was able to discharge his weapon. The surge grazed Sasha's cheek leaving a track of fire across her face. Her claws found their mark, though, and blood gushed out of the men spraying her across their face. She'd hit an artery on one man and he was writhing on the ground as he bled out. The second man's arm fell useless at his side, using his other he tried to get off another shot, but she leaped on top of him. Her teeth closed around his throat and she ripped it out.

Blood poured from her mouth and the human side buried deep inside her brain was screaming at her to stop, but she wasn't finished yet. These people had all but murdered her mate, their bond grew fainter and fainter with each passing minute and the only way to save him was to escape and get help.

Turning back down the length of the hall she could hear marching boots, they were too far away and the hall was too dark for her to see how many were coming. She let out a roar and the narrow corridor amplified the sound, filling the space with her rage. The boots stopped and out of the darkness a lone figure approached. She turned to fully face her new target, her claws were out and her teeth barred prepared to kill who stood between her and saving Dax.

"Sasha, it's me. You need to calm down, we're here to save you."

It was Amiri's voice, but could she trust him? He'd allowed Dax to be taken, it was his fault they were in this position. She growled at her brother.

"I can help you, Sasha. We had a tracker on you, we were able to record everything that was said. I didn't tell you about it because I didn't know how you would react. We have Ariel in custody. Just calm down."

Furious at him for his deception, she roared again. He knew what they had done to Dax and he'd done nothing to stop it.

"Sasha we can still save Dax."

Her human side pushed to the front of her mind and the mist of change covered her. When it was gone Sasha stood naked in front of her brother, covered in blood and a long mean gash crossed her face from her hairline to her chin. "Save him please Amiri, he's dying."

Gesturing to men behind him a team ran past. Her brother walked toward her, he was decked out in fatigues and took off his jacket to hand to her. Her nose wrinkled at his scent, she really didn't want to wrap it around her, she was still angry at him, but standing there naked wasn't an option. Slipping her arms in the sleeves she caught sight of all the blood on her. The lighting was dim, but it was enough for her to see that she was covered. She took a deep breath and that was the worst thing she could have done.

Heaving she bent over and emptied her stomach on Amiri's boots. Wiping her mouth, she tried not to think about what had happened, what she'd done to those men. Sasha was hardly a pacifist, but she'd never killed anyone before. Reaching out to steady her Amiri placed his hand on her arm. Yanking away from him an inhuman snarl came from her lips, "Don't touch me. If he dies I'll never forgive you."

Looking sad he replied, "If he dies I'll never forgive myself."

Chapter Twenty

Standing in the corner, out of everyone's way, Sasha watched as a medical team worked on Dax. Their technology was amazing, but he was so close to death she had no idea if they could help.

"We've stabilized him, he's too badly injured to use the porter we need to get him on a transport and to the nearest hospital."

In seconds, a stretcher was out and they were carrying Dax down the hall. Running after them, out of the corner of her eye Sasha spotted one of the previously closed doors that was now open. Jerking to a halt she looked on in horror as she saw row after row of cots with people strapped to them. Military personnel were walking through the rows inspecting people, but they weren't letting them go.

Stepping forward she planned to start loosening straps when she got her first close look and realized that the man on the bed was already dead. What was worse was the obvious signs of experimentation. His arm and legs had been replaced with someone else's. The open dead eyes staring back at her were different shapes and colors.

"Oh my god, what were they doing here?"

"They were trying to combine different species

to make hybrid animals. Whenever an Andovian mates, their children are shifters from the dominate side. So if a bear and a cat mate the more dominate of the two will be what their children turn into. They were trying to make hybrids in the crudest way imaginable."

Looking up at her brother she asked, "Did you know? I thought Ariel was just trying to take over the kingdom, I didn't realize she was experimenting on people."

"She wasn't, she aligned herself with some very evil people. Thanks to you, though, we've been able to stop them."

"It wasn't soon enough, all these people died because she wanted to be Queen. It's horrible."

Taking her hand, Amiri led her away from the labs. They walked by room after room of people strapped to cots. It wasn't until they got closer to the entrance that she started to hear survivors, but there were so few.

Her bond to Dax had stabilized, but what if that was temporary? What if they weren't able to save him? Her lioness perked up and tried to take over, but Sasha wouldn't let her. She tried to pull herself out of the depression and think positive thoughts, but it didn't work.

Leading her to a porting pad Amiri said, "I'll send you straight to the hospital, one of my guards will be there waiting for you. He'll take you to Dax."

Looking down at her bloody tear streaked face he tried to think of something comforting to say but all he could come up with was, "Dax is strong, I'm sure he'll pull through."

A surge of anger took over and Sasha's fist connected with his eye, completely caught unawares

Amiri fell down at her feet. Standing over him, her teeth bared and eyes blazing with rage she said, "Don't you dare try and cheer me up. This happened because of you. If he dies it's because you didn't tell us what was really going on, you didn't give us a chance to weigh the risks. We would have still helped you, but we would have been more cautious and Dax might not be dying right now."

"Sasha…"

"You will not speak to me. If I ever chose to forgive you I will let you know, until that day I don't want to hear your voice."

Stepping into the porter she confirmed the address Amiri had already put it. The last thing she saw before materializing in the hospital was Amiri's shocked face.

The hospital was a lot like an Earth hospital. It had a very distinct antiseptic smell that was intertwined with the scent of pain and fear. The guard waiting for her led her to the intensive care unit, the closer they got the more another scent started to become clear. It was the distinct odor of death. Her sensitive nose could smell it over everything and her heart clenched in fear.

Arriving at a nurses station Sasha was too afraid to ask Dax's status. Sensing her apprehension, the guard asked for her. They were told he was still in surgery and sent to a waiting room. The guard started to argue, asking for a more private place for Sasha to stay, but she stopped him. It didn't matter where she was and she saw no reason to make things more difficult for the staff.

Finding an open seat in the surprisingly full waiting room, she tried to distract herself. Hours later she had flipped through every entertainment tablet available and was in the middle of a cold war with a teenager that kept hogging the viewer controller. If she had to watch another episode of something called Fang Friends she was going to scream.

When her name was paged she stood up on shaky feet and made it back to the nurses' station where a doctor was waiting for her.

"Your highness, your mate lost a lot of blood and is going to have to spend a considerable amount of time in the regeneration tanks, but he's going to make a full recovery."

Sobbing she pulled the doctor into a tight hug. "Thank you so much. Thank you. Can I see him now?"

Letting go, she could tell she'd embarrassed the doctor but didn't care. She was so happy. She'd been positive that Dax was going to die. He'd been so broken and there had been so much blood. Concentrating she could feel their bond had strengthened. Dax didn't seem to be in pain anymore though he did feel a bit fuzzy.

"Your highness has anyone looked at your injury?"

"What?" She'd completely forgotten the burn across her face, reaching up she felt the hard ridges where her skin had puckered up from the wound. It hurt, but not as much as she thought it should.

"The weapon cauterized the cut so you didn't lose much blood. We can put you through a round in the regeneration tanks, but you'll always have a scar."

"Really?"

Clearing his throat the doctor answered, "It's a battle wound isn't it? Battle wounds are worn with pride your highness. You fought your enemy and came out victorious."

"It is and you're right. I'm sorry, it's been a busy night and I'm a bit out of it. Can I please see Dax?"

"Yes, of course, your highness."

Leading her through the halls they entered a warmly lit room that had a large tank in the center, floating in the tank was Dax. He looked…whole. All the blood and gore was gone, his bones where were they should be, not poking out. There were long gashes and puckered areas where injuries had healed, but he looked so much better.

Moving forward she placed her hand on the tank where his was floating. He was out cold, but she could feel through their bond that he knew she was there and was happy. Resting her forehead on the tank she breathed out and fought back tears. She'd survived her first few days on Andove, hopefully, the rest to come were less action packed.

Three days later Dax and Sasha were finished with their regeneration sessions. She had a red scar across one side of her face, but Dax assured her it just made her look sexier. She wasn't sure about that but decided not to let it bother her. His scars were less noticeable and they didn't make her want him any less. They were being summoned to the palace, but Sasha wanted to stop off at Dax's apartment first and try and communicate with Anika.

They were days past the time they were supposed to check in and Sasha was concerned about what had happened while they'd been out of contact. Had they found Kelly yet? Had they been able to save her? Before she faced whatever else her family had to throw at her she had to know what was going on with her friend.

Entering the apartment, Dax said, "It will just take a minute. My communication system is top of the line and shouldn't have any issue connecting with the ship."

He paused when he got to the panel. It was blinking red and flashing an urgent communication warning. Concerned he looked over his shoulder at Sasha before playing the message.

Anika's face filled the screen. Dirt was smudged all across her face, her hair was a mess, and most worrisome of all there was a bloody wound across her forehead. They could hear Zeke in the background cursing, and the ship shook from the force of a direct hit. The shield integrity was announced and Anika's message was rushed.

"Sasha we need your help. We found Kelly and were able to rescue her from the auction house, but shit happened and now we don't know where she or Klews are. We've narrowed it down to a few planets, but the Hunters have found us and we're under attack."

The ship took another hit and Anika disappeared from the screen. They could hear Zeke screaming at her that they had to jump to hyperspace now. Her head popped back into view and their coordinates flashed across the screen.

"Help Sasha, please."

The screen went blank. Dax's hands flew across the panel as he tried to connect with the ship but it was no use, they didn't answer. The message was over four days old, there was no telling where they were now. All they had were the coordinates that Anika had transmitted to them.

"Oh my god Dax, what are we going to do?"

Keep Reading for a Free Preview of Hunted

*Book Three in the Twin Moons of Andove
Now Available!*

Author's Note

Thanks for reading "Stolen", I hope you enjoyed Sasha and Dax's story. It looks like their friends are in some real danger, "Hunted" is the next book in the Twin Moons of Andove.

If you enjoyed this story, one of the best things you can do is leave a review.
If you would like to be notified of future installments in the series please sign up for my mailing list.

CassandraLogan.com

Free Sneak Peek of *Hunted*
Book Three in the Twin Moons of Andove

Huddling in the center of a tall cage Kelly tried not to cry. The last time Ajax caught sight of her tear streaked face he'd gone into a rage and slapped her hard enough to leave a bright red mark. Standing over her crumpled form he'd grabbed her by the hair and said, "If I see you crying again I'll give you something to cry about."

Throwing her to the ground she'd whimpered but somehow managed to keep the tears from falling. She had no idea what was happening. She'd been asleep in her parent's home when she felt a tingling sensation and then she was in a small room with two other women. The scary one kept growling and had super sharp teeth and bright blue eyes. The other woman seemed nice enough and Kelly clung to her words that everything would be okay.

Sasha. That was her name. She had seemed so calm and collected and like she could take care of everyone. Kelly held tightly to the tiny sliver of hope that Sasha would find her and rescue her from this horrible place.

Eyes burning she fought to control the tears she felt at her desperate situation. Things were made only worse when she was bombarded with sound waves. They felt like hands caressing her body and it made her sick inside. Biting her lip, a single tear fell from her eye. Quickly brushing it aside she hoped Ajax hadn't seen. As quickly as the sound waves began they stopped. Shivering she stood up, her nightgown clung to her body, and she wished she'd been wearing her flannels when she'd been abducted.

"Much better. The stench of that god awful planet was beginning to make me sick. Now put this on."

Ajax tossed her a thin, slinky dress and leered at her. Holding it with just the tips of her fingers she shook her head vigorously, "No."

Growling he flipped a switch on a remote he carried with him everywhere. The cage lit up and a painful electric shock coursed through her body. A squeal escaped her lips and her feet danced as she tried to keep them off the floor. When the shocks stopped her body was tingling, but thankfully that seemed to be the worst of it.

"Put it on or the next time it will be worse."

Shivering she slipped the flimsy dress over her head. It stopped just beneath her butt and dipped low in the front. Her breasts were large and the dress was tight against them.

"I'm growing impatient Kelly. Take off your other clothes or I'll light your cage up like it's Christmas."

Her hands jerked as she pulled her arms in and began taking her nightgown off. Tossing it through the bars she crossed her arms over her chest and glared at Ajax.

"The rest too."

"What?!"

"Buyers want to see what they're purchasing and Andovians are known for their enjoyment of their naked form."

"Well, I'm not Andovian."

"I hate to break it to you sweetheart, but you're not from Earth. I took you from your real parents when you were just a baby and brought you to that hell hole in the middle of fucking nowhere. I needed time for you to grow up and someplace I wouldn't be found. Those people that raised you lied to you your entire life. You aren't their child."

At the mention of her parents, sadness enveloped her, but anger quickly pushed it aside. "My parents never lied to me. I knew I was adopted and that didn't matter because they love me."

He snorted at that, "Whatever lets you sleep at night. Now take off the rest of your clothes."

His finger hovered over the remote button and she pushed her underwear down. Pulling her arms through her bra straps she unhooked the back and her breasts dropped without the support. Sitting down in the middle of the cage she tried to get the dress to cover as much of her body as possible, but the cool breeze she felt on the top of her butt let her know she was failing.

Burying her head in her knees she ignored Ajax's disgusting comments. She focused on her family. She'd known all her life she was adopted, but it had never been a big deal. Her brother was adopted too. Her family wasn't perfect, but they were perfect for her. Laughter and teasing reigned supreme in her home growing up and she could really use some of that right now.

The room she was being held in grew silent as Ajax left her alone. Shivering again, this time from the cold, she rubbed her hands up and down her arms trying to warm them up. Looking around, making sure no one was there, she stood up and started pacing in the cell to get her blood pumping.

She wasn't sure how long she'd been locked up, maybe a week, maybe longer. She would kill for some room to stretch. She'd always been athletic, spending hours at the gym each week, and she missed the exercise. She missed a lot of things.

Tears came back to well up in her eyes. She was never going to escape, there was just no way. She'd tested the bars and they weren't moving. There didn't even appear to be a door, at least not any kind of locking mechanism. She was going to be sold to some kind of hunter. Ajax had taken great pleasure in telling her what they would do to her.

Bile came up her throat as she remembered all he'd told her. They liked to rape their Andovian slaves and then hunt them in their animal form. She wasn't sure what some of that meant, but she really didn't like the sound of any of it.

Kelly had never thought of herself as a coward, however, she'd never been in a situation where she had to defend herself. Any time she'd ever come up against a tough situation she'd always had her family to lean on. No matter what happened she knew they would be there to protect and help her, except now. She was alone and it didn't matter what Sasha had told her, she knew no one was going to rescue her and she wasn't strong enough to rescue herself.

Unable to think about what was about to happen she focused on what else Ajax had said, she was

Andovian. What did that mean? Clearly she was no longer on Earth when they'd moved her from her first cell, which was really just a small dark room, to her current location, she'd seen space outside. As in stars and blackness and nothing else. She had moved through air locks and the people on the other side hadn't been people. At least not human.

She shivered again at the thought of what had greeted her. After days of only seeing Ajax, a short horrible man that loved leering at her and pinching her cheeks, she was met with an impossibly tall, blue, bald man that had an entourage of short fuzzy monster like creatures. His voice had been so deep she had felt it in her chest. Booming it hit her ears with force and somehow she'd understood everything he said.

Absentmindedly she rubbed her arms as she remembered how he had spoken like she didn't matter, like selling someone was normal.

"You're late Ajax. The auction is in a few hours and we don't have enough time to add you to the docket."

"Cool it, Bluebeard. It will be worth the added work, I've got a virgin Andovian."

Sniffing at her Bluebeard said, "I thought you were supposed to be bringing three of them."

Turning red Ajax blustered, "One Andovian is better than none. You know, even with the short notice, once you announce you have a virgin Andovian female your attendance will double. Especially since we're this close to the Hunter's homeworld."

Bluebeard responded, "We shall see. We have to process her first." His eyes swept over Kelly and he shook his head before turning and walking away.

Ajax had been furious. He dragged her behind

him, nearly pulling her arm out of its socket, and screamed at her the entire way. He threw her into the cell she now occupied and then left her alone.

Kelly had always believed that aliens were out there, but she'd never thought she'd get this up close and personal to them. Shivering again she increased her pacing but it wasn't helping. The dress, if it could even be called that, was just too thin and provided no warmth. Looking past the bars at the large empty room she was in she worried about what was going to happen next.

Once again, she tried to block out what Ajax had told her, but his words kept surfacing in her mind. He'd told her over and over again what was going to be done to her and even after all that repetition it wasn't until she'd met Bluebeard that she believed it could be true. Hunters were going to buy her, rape her, and then release her on a strange planet, only to be hunted down and murdered.

How was she supposed to survive something like that? She wasn't, that was the point. Hiccupping she fought back tears. She was going to die a horrible, awful death, and there was nothing she could do about it. Nothing.

About the Author

Cassandra Logan lives in central North Carolina with her husband, daughter, and their two cats. When she's not writing she spends her time reading, binge watching Netflix, and baking sinfully delicious deserts.

She is the author of the Nians on Earth series and the Twin Moons of Andove series. She is currently working on expanding the Twin Moons of Andove and Nian universe.

CassandraLogan.com

Twin Moons of Andove Character List

Afua Levon, King- Lion shifter, his greatest regret is the loss of his oldest daughter.

Ajax- A small time con artist that graduated to kidnapping and trafficking when he got a hold of the Feline royal princess and then grabbed two more girls to sweeten the deal.

Akali 'Sasha' Levon, Princess- Lioness shifter that was kidnapped from her family at a young age. She was raised in a series of foster homes and had no idea what she was until Zeke mated with Anika.

Amiri Levon, Prince- Lion shifter, he is known for his violent temper but has worked very hard to keep it under control. Active in the Feline military and training to one day take over the role of king

Anika- Wolf shifter that was kidnapped and raised by a man she thought was her uncle, Ajax

Ariel Levon, Ambassador- Lioness shifter, she is sister to King Afua, she is a very cold woman that feels slighted by the Feline rules of ascension and her place in the family.

Dax- Panther shifter, he was dishonorably discharged from the Feline Royal Military for something he did not do.

Henri Klews- Bear shifter that has a problem going berserk, he tends to avoid violent situations by staying on the ship that he co-owns with Zeke and Dax

Kelly- Ajax's third kidnapped victim she is currently being held hostage and has no idea what's going on.

Laini Levon, Princess- Lioness shifter, she is a few years younger than Sasha and has lived her whole life under the shadow of her abduction. Despite that she is sweet and loving and very happy to have her sister back.

Layla Levon, Queen- Lioness shifter, she is a kind, gentle woman and was the only thing that kept the king from going crazy searching for Sasha.

Yolanda- Bear shifter, she is the head chef for the Feline Royal family

Zeke- Wolf shifter that falls in love and mates Anika in the book Abducted. He co-owns a salvage ship with his two best friends, Klews and Dax.

Series Information

Twin Moons of Andove
Book One: "Abducted"
Book Two: "Stolen"
Book Three: "Hunted"
Book Four: "Deception"

Nians on Earth
Book Zero: "Nians on Earth Prequel"
Book One: "Destiny"
Book Two: "Desire"
Book Three: "Delight"
Book Four: "Deception"

The Fringes of the Universe
Book One: "Guiding Light"
Book Two: COMING SOON!

Standalone Stories
Santa's Scrooge: A Christmas Short Story
Witches of Cadence Cove Shorts Vol. 1